Tales of Adventure #1

A Compilation of Five Short Novels

Michael Kingswood

Tales of Adventure #1

A Compilation of Five Short Novels

Michael Kingswood

Additional Works

Table Of Contents

Passing In The Night

One

S pace travel sucks sometimes.

The thought crossed through Carlton's mind as, for the three-hundredth time this shift, he checked the navigation display. Just as it almost always did, the ship's position tracked exactly with projections.

Terribly boring.

But then, that was to be expected of interstellar travel. With hundreds of thousands of Astronomical Units - AUs - to cover, even a relatively short trip could take years. Unfortunately, this was no short trip. The run from the Gliese system to Earth, though routine, was also 20.5 light years in length. Even at the ship's cruising speed of 95% of the speed of light (.95c), it would take almost six and a half years to complete the trip. Of course, it took a little less than a year to get up to cruising speed, and a another year to slow back down again, so the total trip was closer to ten years. But it could be worse. Without the time dilation caused by relativity, it would be almost twenty-five years.

God bless Einstein.

It was just rotten luck that Carlton drew this portion of the trip. The center passage was mind numbingly dull: nothing much to do for the year but monitor instruments and readouts and maybe make a slight course correction every now and then. Which is why it paid the least. But everyone drew the short stick sometimes.

He tapped the upper right corner of the display, and it shifted from Navigation to Engineering. Another tap pulled up the reactor specs.

Located two kilometers aft of the crewed area of the ship to save on shielding material, the reactor was an old-style fission device. Newer ships had fusion generators these days, of course. But construction on Pericles completed two years before Kilpatrick and Holbert patented the containment device that made fusion practical, and there was no point in scrapping a new and perfectly capable ship just because some new tech came along.

So the Company put Pericles in service on the Gliese run. This was her fourth transit of the interstellar void. When they reached earth, it would be time for her hundred-year overhaul.

That didn't make a whole lot of sense to Carlton. Sure, Pericles would be about a hundred Earth years old when they docked, but she had only experienced a little less than 40 years of time-dilated service. No one asked him, though. He was just the driver.

The reactor specs all fell in the normal range. No surprise there, considering that without the plasma generators online to power the main engines, the reactor put out just a small fraction of its rated power.

Carlton moved on to life support.

Again, everything read normal. Consumables were depleting as expected. The crops in the hydroponics section were looking good, and the waste reclamation system was churning along nicely. Carlton expect this, as the system was operating at much less than its maximum capacity.

Next, gravity.

The crewed section of the ship consisted of two rings, each a kilometer in diameter and fifty meters wide, with three decks. They connected to the central hub of the ship through four passage tubes, and rotated continually in opposite directions during cruise flight to simulate gravity. During acceleration to and deceleration from cruise speed, the main engines provided all the G forces necessary.

Though initially set to simulate Gliese-normal gravity, the computer system slowly lowered the rotation period so that, at the end of the journey, gravity would be reduced to Earth-normal. The slow transition made it easy for the crew and passengers to acclimate to their new environs before arrival. That was one good thing about these longer passages. The passage from the Centauri colony was short enough for the transition to be difficult for some people. None of that trouble on the Gliese run, though.

Accelerometers in each section of A and B rings sent readouts to the display monitor. 10.36 m/sec2. Right on track.

Carlton pulled up cryogenics.

Cryo was the most important system on the ship, at least to the eggheads at Corporate. Five thousand passengers, plus the rest of the crew aside from Carlton's shift, peacefully slept away the cruise under cryo-suspension, with periodically programmed massage and movement sessions. Cryo-suspension did not completely stop metabolic processes, after all. The nearly ten year passage would be equivalent to about six months of normal aging: long enough for the passengers to suffer severe muscle atrophy if they were not kept in motion periodically. They, and the cargo in the holds, were the reason Carlton was here. Their fares paid his commission, so he supposed cryo was the most important system for him, too.

He chuckled at that thought.

Just one last thing to check. Carlton punched up the external sensors and began a scan.

First, the hull monitoring cameras. Again as usual, he found no blemishes on the hull.

Next, the forward looking scanners. Pericles had radar units, of course, but at her current speed, by the time they received the returns, they would be almost on any objects in their path. And while starliners were equipped with exterior coils that generated a magnetic field to repel charged particles, the field did nothing for solid objects. Even a tiny object could create a fatal collision at relativistic speeds. The destruction of the Avalon, one of the first transport vessels to the Gliese system, was reportedly caused by a collision with a meteor the size of a melon.

To help defend against that, and to assist with navigation, the Company deployed and maintained a quartet of beacons every few light-hours along the spacelanes between the various colonies. Every starliner carried a few beacons to replace units that were approaching end of life or whose orbit had carried them too far from the most efficient course between stars. Pericles had just three days earlier deployed four to replace an aging quartet. The beacons transmitted coded radio signals. Pericles carried receiver units tuned for them, and could use the signals to help triangulate her position as well as detect objects ahead by interpolating the interference patterns between the signals from the beacons. It was a pretty efficient system, all things considered.

It took just a second to update the ahead display after Carlton shifted over from the cameras. There were no objects of concern within the next four hours of travel. Satisfied, Carlton set the automatic monitoring system to issue an alert if it detected anything, then pushed back from his console.

The bridge was smaller than a lay person might expect for a ship Pericles' size: just a pilot station, a communications panel, and a command console for the Captain, all situated in a small bubble atop the hull, with viewing windows in all directions. The Captain's station was astern and above the others. All were nestled between stairs leading back to the aft bulkhead, where the hatch to the rest of the ship nestled in the floor. During acceleration, crewmembers could walk up the stairs to sit in the chairs, their backs to the G forces.

Carlton could have run the diagnostic programs from a workstation in the command center down in the crew quarters, but he rather enjoyed coming up here. For one thing, it had some of the only windows on the ship without a rotating view. It was nice to be able to look at one point in space without losing it after a few seconds.

Of course, the view at cruising speed was different, disconcerting to the un-initiated. The light from the stars ahead was so blueshifted that very little was actually visible to the eye. The stars astern were redshifted similarly. But looking athwartships one could almost think one was looking up at a normal night sky from the surface of a planet somewhere.

Almost.

The other thing he enjoyed was being in zero-G. No matter how many times he experienced it, Carlton never quite got over how different, and fun, it was. Some people got space sick from being in zero-G for too long, but he never had. He almost wished he could spend the whole trip like this. But he wasn't a big fan of losing all muscle tone and getting brittle bones, so he did not wish too hard.

Carlton only lingered for a moment before pushing himself through the hatch to the central corridor of the hub.

Handholds on the walls made for easy travel through the bulkheads and hatches that separated the bridge from the crew's acceleration quarters, and then through more bulkheads to the junction with Ring A, two hundred meters aft. During acceleration, the handholds would be ladder rungs, and the corridor a vertical shaft between decks. Yes, it was much more fun moving around during cruise, in zero-G.

At the junction, he took a moment to locate the tunnel to section four. It was always a bit annoying getting into the lift, with the hatch rotating around the junction, but he managed it without too much trouble.

The hatch slid shut behind him, and Carlton found himself pressed up against one wall as the ring's rotation met his body and carried it along. Positioning himself feet "down", toward the ring itself, he pushed himself to what would be the lift's floor once the G's began to build up and pushed the button for the first deck.

Ring A, Section Four, First Deck was crew quarters. The rest of Ring A contained consumables storage, hydroponics, life support equipment, and passenger berthing. Ring B was completely taken up with cargo storage. As with buildings planetside, the rings' decks were numbered from bottom to top, so the first deck was the outermost and the third deck the innermost on the ring.

It took two and a half minutes to descend the five hundred meters to the first deck. By then, Jack's feet were planted firmly on the floor, and he felt normal gravity, or at least a close approximation. If he threw a ball, it would not fly exactly the same way it would in a real gravity well, but it was close enough to do the job.

The lift door opened, and he stepped out into a small al-cove, recessed in the aft wall of the main corridor. The wall directly opposite the lift door was terraced, almost like stairs turned on their sides.

Stepping into the corridor itself, Carlton noted as usual how it curved upward noticeably in each direction. The cor-ridor was tiled in light brown tiles that, barring close inspec-tion, were easy to mistake for wood. Faux-wood panels on the walls and softly glowing light fixtures at regular intervals combined with potted plants every so often gave the passage a somewhat homey feel. Prints of various artwork hung on the walls as well, except on the lift side of the corridor, to the left. During acceleration, the changing crew shifts could walk up the stairs in the wall from the lift, then down the corridor to the crew's cryo-suspension beds.

Newcomers to space travel might be surprised at the decor, very much like a nice hotel, but researchers long ago dis-covered that the more comfortable people were in their living quarters, the less stressful they found long duration space flight. For the passengers, this was not a concern. They entered cryo-suspension not long after boarding, before the ship actually got underway, and awoke after the ship moored. But the crew had to live aboard, so starliner designers tried to make their living arrangements as close to luxury as they could.

Carlton found the Duty Captain in the command center, fifty meters down the corridor to the right. She was sitting at her desk near the back of the room, dressed in the light grey coveralls that all starliner crewmembers wore underway and sipping on a cup of coffee as she watched the news feed on a view screen.

The news came across on the coded signal from the

beacons. While it was very time late, it helped morale to have some notion of what was going on at their destination. It beat showing up to the planet and having no idea of recent history on the ground.

Seeing her alone, Carlton grunted. "Where is everyone?"

The Captain shrugged. "Bryce went off to fix a problem in the galley. Malcolm and Stephanie are helping teach science class."

Bryce was one of the two general technicians on the shift. Malcolm was the shift engineer, and Stephanie one of the reactor techs.

Each shift manned the ship for one year of the passage, and was kept as small as possible. In general, a shift consisted of the Duty Captain, two pilots, the shift engineer, two reactor techs, the doctor, two cooks, two horticulturists, and the teacher. Plus the crew's children. The pilots, techs, and cooks swapped twelve hour watches. The others were on call as needed, but generally worked a normal day.

"Ah. Well everything looks good. Right on the money." Carlton walked over to her desk to get a better look at the view screen. "Anything interesting going on?"

"More riots in Brazil. Looks like it's getting pretty bad."

"Well, it's nothing we need to worry about. If you need me, I'll be helping Alison."

"Right."

It became very obvious, in the earliest of humanity's excursions to the stars over five hundred years ago, that it was asking far too much for a person to leave family behind while embarking on a decades-long journey. By the time a starfarer returned from even a short trip, he would have missed much of his kids' childhood, to say nothing of the toll it took on marriages.

So almost from the beginning, crewmembers brought their

families with them. Large as the starliners were, though, extraneous personnel were a burden, so family members learned tasks to assist in running the ships. Case in point, Alison was Carlton's wife, and the shift's doctor.

Eventually, the crews of the various ships became more extended families than colleagues, and the starfarers developed a culture altogether unique from the ground-based. Entire generations were born, lived, and died working on the starliners. Sure, some crewmembers left after their initial contracts expired, deciding they preferred life planetside. And some children opted for a different life as well. But for the most part, starfarers were a distinct clan.

Like him, Alison was raised on a starliner. They met on shore leave five years ago. When it came time for her to ship out again, he arranged a transfer onto Pericles to be with her. The rest, as they say, was history.

Carlton found her in the clinic, taking an inventory of the various drugs in storage. Managing medical supplies was tricky on long voyages. Drug expiration had to be carefully tracked, and fresh supplies removed from cryo-freeze early to avoid any gaps in availability during the long thawing process. Carlton did not envy her that.

Alison looked up as Carlton entered and beamed at him. "A letter from Sasha came over a few minutes ago. He got into Harvard Med!"

Sasha was her younger brother, stationed on another starliner on the Gliese route. Family members who were not on the same ship almost always worked to remain on the same route. It often worked out that they were able to see each other on shore leave on one side of the route or other. With the time compression of cryo-suspension, that generally worked out to seeing each other every three or four waking years, for a few months at a time.

Carlton returned Alison's smile. "That's great! When does he start school?"

"They're four earth-years ahead of us on the route, so he should be just about finishing when we arrive."

"Just in time for graduation. That should be a good party."

Alison nodded. "And we're rolling to shore duty, so we can be there for his residency."

Shore duty. It was both cherished and dreaded.

Starfarers got leave at the end of each run while maintenance crews worked on the ship. Depending on how much was planned for the upkeep, they could get anywhere from three to six months off. But this run was different. Pericles' overhaul was scheduled to take almost four years. That was too long for the crew to do nothing, so typically they were assigned to train new hires or manage projects at the corporate headquarters. It was good, in a sense. Being in one place for a while had its advantages.

But a body could grow soft, too. Especially for people with children in their teen years, being ashore that long carried its own worries. Most children who opted out of the starfarers' life were teenagers planetside on shore duty. They lost their love for the ships during that time and left, leaving their parents with an impossible choice: to leave the lives they loved or the kids they loved.

That's why most of the short-hop starliners were manned with older crews. The crewmembers could continue their jobs, but still see their kids every few earth years. It was a compromise many made that seemed to work out. Fortunately for Carlton and Alison, their son was only three, so that worry was a long way off, still.

Carlton was about to respond when the first few bars from Beethoven's Fifth Symphony emanated from the console on the wall and drew his attention. Each crewmember wore locator devices that allowed the ship's internal sensors to keep track of them and forward calls wherever they were onboard. Beethoven's Fifth was Carlton's "ring tone", to borrow a phrase from ancient Earth history.

He walked over to the console and tapped the screen. An automated message popped up. Forward sensors had detected something ahead.

Carlton frowned in annoyance. Probably just another rogue asteroid crossing their path. All the same, he had to check it out.

"I gotta go back to the bridge, babe. Be back in a bit."

Five minutes later, he floated up to his pilot's console and woke it up with a tap on the screen. A couple taps later he had the forward sensors called up.

This was no asteroid.

Whatever it was, it was big, about a light-hour ahead, and traveling on a near-collision course with them. The doppler readout indicated the object was traveling at .8c: slower than a starliner, but definitely not natural.

Carlton punched up the intercom to the command center.

"Yeah Carl. What's up?"

"Better get up here, Cap'n."

In the few minutes it took the Captain to get to the bridge, Carlton entered the commands to wake up the lower forward observation camera. Essentially a 4 meter telescope mounted beneath the bow of the ship, the camera, and its fellows mounted just aft of the bridge and above and below the main engines' fuel tanks aft, was onboard for just this purpose.

The camera finished warming up and was beginning to zoom in on the approaching object when the Captain arrived at his side.

"Object ahead, Cap'n. Moving too fast to be an asteroid."

Her eyes scanned the sensor readout quickly, and she nodded agreement.

"Another starliner?"

"Not supposed to be another until Haverly, next month. Besides, this thing's too slow."

"Maybe…"

The Captain's words stuck in her throat as the image from the camera filled the screen.

It was difficult to make out in the faint illumination from the distant stars, but it was definitely a vessel. It was of no design Carlton had ever seen, though, and he had seen them all. No rings, no plasma engine nacelles. It was crescent-shaped, off-white in color, and tumbled slowly end over end through space.

"What the hell is that?" Carlton breathed.

The Captain was silent for a long minute, her expression one of curiosity.

"What's the CPA?"

"Wait one." Carlton tapped the display, and the data came up. "Closest Point of Approach: .75 AU, Bearing 328 mark 47, in one hour, seven minutes." A CPA above Pericles and to the left explained why he did not detect the vessel earlier. Though it was in their plane of travel now, it must have drifted up from below.

"Hmm. On that trajectory, it didn't come from Earth. Any other colonies out that way?"

Carlton shook his head. Even before calling up the nav display, he knew the answer.

"Closest is Talos, but that thing's forty degrees off course to have come from there."

There was a long silence as they watched the strange ship grow slowly larger on the camera display. Carlton knew the Captain was thinking the same thing as he, but it was too incredible to voice.

"Maybe whatever crippled it knocked it off course."

The Captain snorted.

"What do we do?"

Pushing herself away from the pilot's console, the Captain floated to the starboard side viewing window. She looked out at the passing stars for a while.

Carlton alternated between watching her and the approaching ship. He knew better than to press too hard, though. When she got pensive like this, the Captain could be snippy.

Eventually, she spoke, in the tone she used when she really meant business.

"Keep watching it, and let me know if anything changes. Be sure to record everything. I'm going below to check on a couple things, but I'll be back before it reaches CPA."

With that, she pushed off and floated back to the entrance hatch. Before she disappeared below, she issued a final order.

"Keep this quiet, Carl. Lock out the workstations in the ring, and don't breathe a word to anyone until I get back."

Carlton blinked. Lock out the workstations? That was almost unheard of. What was she worried about? This was potentially huge! Everyone would want to know. Would deserve to know. But he had flown with the Captain for a lot of years, and had learned to trust her judgment. Obediently, he keyed the commands to restrict access.

Two

For the next forty-five minutes, Carlton watched the strange ship draw nearer.

As it grew in the display, he made out more details. Strange markings, letters of some kind he thought, but in no language he had ever seen, decorated the hull in a number of places. The hull was breached. Twin cuts, perfectly parallel and framed with dark scorch marks, tore across the vessel's port side. Gasses of some variety or other vented to space through the cuts, slowly increasing the ship's rate of rotation. Whatever happened to that ship, it had occurred recently.

True to her word, the Captain returned to the bridge. As she floated up to the pilot's console, Carlton noticed she had a spiral-bound stack of paper tucked under her arm. Paper! Carlton hadn't seen a paper document since...well, come to think of it, he had never seen a paper document. He had heard of people who kept paper books in libraries, collectors and the like. But he did not have that kind of money. Nor did anyone he knew.

"Any change, Carl?"

"Nope. But take a look at this."

Carlton tapped the screen, pausing the image as the twin cuts on the vessel's hull rotated into view.

"Those look like plasma burns to me."

The Captain pursed her lips, nodding in agreement. She leaned forward a bit, peering intently at the image on the screen. As she did, the papers under her arm shifted a bit, and Carlton saw "TOP SECRET: CAPTAIN'S EYES ONLY" written at the top of the title page.

"What's so secret, Cap'n?"

She pulled back, covering the pages up with her free hand for a heartbeat. Then, seeing the knowing look in Carlton's eyes, she sighed and withdrew the papers from under her arm.

"These are procedures to follow in the event a starliner should encounter evidence of intelligent extraterrestrial life."

Carlton's eyebrow twitched upward, but before he could say a word, the Captain wagged a finger at him.

"You never saw these papers, Carl. Understand? It's both our asses, otherwise."

"Come on, Cap'n. What're they gonna…"

She leaned forward, a fierce light in her eyes.

"I'm not screwing around, Carl. We could both disappear if we mess this up."

She tapped a finger on the bottom of the title page, drawing Carl's eye. His protests died on his lips when he saw the name there. Though officially denied, it was common knowledge that the NSA did just that with inconvenient people. He swallowed, despite the fact that his mouth had just gone dry.

"Alright, so what are we supposed to do?"

"Keep an accurate record of the entire event. Take no

provocative actions. Send reports to the government."

"You're kidding."

"Huh?"

"That's all stuff we were going to do anyway."

"Well…yeah."

Carlton threw up his hands.

"What the hell's so Top Secret about that?"

The Captain smirked. "Clearly you've never seen classified documents before. The fact that it deals with ETs is what makes it Top Secret." She leaned forward, eyes narrowing as she examined the tumbling ship. "Can you zoom in any further, make this more clear?" She pointed at a single blister-like bubble on the dorsal area of the ship.

Carlton nodded. He tapped on the image, freezing it in place as the bubble rotated into view again. Then with a two-fingered spreading gesture, he activated the display's zoom feature. The image took a few seconds to stabilize. When it resolved, the bubble was more clearly visible. A lone light shone from the bubble, dimly illuminating the forward area of the hull.

"Son of a bitch. It still has power."

"That changes things," said the Captain as she turned toward the communication console. She tapped the console, rousing it from standby, then flipped open her procedure to a page near the back. She frowned, tapping at her lips with her index finger, as she read.

"What are you doing?"

She began tapping on the console, and a screen Carlton had never seen before opened up.

"There are generic communication protocols programmed in the comms system. Peace, friendship, that sort of thing. Procedure states we try to make contact, if possible."

A loud snort was Carlton's initial reply.

"You can't be serious. We don't know what frequencies they use, and…"

The Captain interrupted.

"So we use every frequency we can transmit on."

"Fine, but you can't really think they'll understand, even if they receive it."

The Captain opened her mouth to reply, but he kept on talking.

"And even if they did, it's pointless anyway. We can't exactly do anything to help them."

That much was certain. Pericles carried enough fuel for the initial acceleration, deceleration at the destination star system, and intra-system maneuvering. They could stop to render assistance to the other craft, but doing so would strand them in the interstellar void, making the gesture worse than useless. The Captain knew this as well as he did.

"Understood. Regardless, we're going to follow procedure."

With that, she made one last tap on the communication console, and the antenna status indications lit up across all bands as Pericles began transmitting.

She and Carlton both turned their attention to the camera display. They watched intently for any change in the other vessel. Nothing was forthcoming. The vessel continued tumbling, apparently out of control.

Carlton checked the time. Ten minutes to CPA. The vessel's bearing rate had picked up considerably. Tracking had shifted to the forward upper camera, but very soon it would be unable to maintain track. The vessel was simply moving too fast, and was too close. So he directed the aft upper camera toward the vessel's expected departure bearing, in order to pick up visual tracking after it passed CPA.

Despite his misgivings about the transmission, Carlton felt

disappointment at the lack of response. Though mankind had been traveling the stars for centuries, and had discovered several dozen life-supporting worlds, the holy grail of meeting an intelligent, sentient alien race had eluded them. There had never even been a hint that anyone else was out there. After so long, most people gave up on the notion, accepting that humanity was alone, at least in this corner of Galaxy. And now, suddenly, to be confronted with an apparent alien artifact…it was unbelievable. Exciting.

And scary.

On the display screen, the strange vessel slipped off frame.

"Lost track due to CPA effect, Cap'n."

"Very well. How long to regain on the other side?"

Carlton tapped the display, and it shifted to a 3-D relative motion display with the vessel's dead reckoning position plotted out in one minute increments.

"Estimated six minutes."

The Captain moved herself closer to the port side viewing window and looked out and upward toward the other vessel's position. Of course it was too far away to see with the naked eye, but Carlton understood the need to look.

"Carl, how close will that thing pass to Gliese?"

That computation was more difficult, but it only took a minute or so.

"About half a parsec. Hard to do a salvage at that distance, if that's what you're thinking."

"True, but it's worth making the attempt."

She turned away from the window and looked at Carlton, her expression one of wonder.

"Of all the ways to meet. Do you have any idea what the odds are of just randomly bumping into them like this?"

He nodded. To say the odds were astronomical would be an understatement. And ironic.

"Guess we should buy lottery tickets when we get…"

An alert flashed on the screen. He tapped the dialogue window and the display shifted to the aft upper camera. Carlton was gratified to see the vessel centered in the frame.

"Ok, re-acquired visual track on the aft upper camera. Gain bearing and time match predicted."

The Captain moved back next to Carlton, the better to see the display.

"Is it just me, or did something change?"

Carlton frowned, shaking his head.

"Don't think so. We're looking at a different angle…"

He stopped mid-sentence as suddenly something broke off from the vessel's ventral section. Apparently spherical, the object shot straight away from the vessel for a few seconds, then a purple-blue glow appeared on one side of the object, and it moved to the right until it disappeared off frame.

"What the hell was that?" exclaimed the Captain.

"No idea, Cap'n. Tracking in the forward upper camera."

Carlton split the camera display and directed the idle camera over. It took several moments to gain the smaller object, but finally it appeared in frame. Carlton zoomed in tight and pull out more details.

The object was indeed generally spherical. From its angular size and the mother ship's known range, the computer estimated the object's size: 15 meters in diameter. On the near side, he could see a number of protuberances that held what looked like antennas and other sensors. The glow came from nozzles that were just barely visible on the far side of the object; obviously that was a propulsion system of some sort. A few circular outlines, possibly hatches, graced the surface of the object, as did more of that strange script.

Carlton frowned. "It almost looks like a lifepod."

"Where's it going?" The Captain sounded worried.

For that matter, Carlton was beginning to get a case of nerves, too. They were far away from anything and everything here. There was no place for a lifepod to go…except to the Pericles. But they were moving too fast for a lifepod to catch up.

Weren't they?

Carlton punched up the tracking subroutine and made a few quick computations. He blinked at the results. That couldn't be right. But doing the computations again yielded the same answer.

He cleared his throat. "Ah. Cap'n, based on its change in bearing rate, that thing's decelerating at over ten thousand Gs. If it keeps on like this after it stops, it'll match our forward velocity in just a few minutes."

The Captain's eyebrows climbed high on her forehead.

"How is that possible? That much force would crush that craft and everyone on it!"

"No lie there, Cap'n, but I've run the numbers twice."

"How long until it reaches us?"

Carlton spread his heads helplessly. "Depends how fast it gets. We've got a couple AUs head start. A few hours, probably."

"Son of a…"

A bright flash from the display screen drew their attention once more. The feed from the aft upper camera was whited out for a second while the computer adjusted the camera's gain. When the frame cleared, all that could be seen of the mothership was a rapidly expanding cloud of fragments and heated gas. The vessel had apparently exploded.

Carlton whistled appreciatively.

"Lucky for them they made it off when they did."

"Unless they blew the ship up on purpose."

"Right. Why would they do that?"

The Captain rolled her eyes. "Think about it, Carl. They're probably more advanced than we are. That's a big advantage. They're not going to want to just hand over their ship, with all its technology, for us, or someone else, to reverse engineer."

It had been generations since mankind last warred with itself. But still the memories of the intrigues between nation-states were vivid, kept alive in school as a lesson to the next generation about the foolishness of tribalism and the need to maintain ties between humanity's colonies as close as possible, considering the distances to be traversed. Some organizations, such as the Society for Creative Anachronism, kept the memories alive for entertainment purposes. And of course, businesses still competed against one another, executing their intrigues, very real despite their non-violent nature, in an attempt to gain a competitive edge. So Carl could understand the Captain's logic. It made perfect sense, when he stopped to think about it.

Carlton closed the aft upper camera display, and the life-pod, if that's what it was, filled the entire screen.

"Won't be able to keep this quiet when that thing comes knocking, Cap'n."

"Don't I know it." The Captain exhaled loudly. "Ask Alison to come up, Carl."

He blinked in surprise.

"Say again?"

"Your wife. Have her come up here. Now."

She was back into her no-nonsense voice again. Carlton keyed the intercom, and a moment later Alison answered.

"You've been up there a while. Everything alright?"

"Yeah. Can you come up?"

She didn't answer for several seconds. When she did, she sounded worried.

"What's wrong, honey?"

"Nothing. Just come up please."

The connection closed, and Carlton and the Captain floated in silence, watching the camera display.

Carlton used the time to compute the lifepod's predicted course, and was not surprised to find it on an intercept trajectory. By the time Alison arrived on the bridge, it had completely stopped its motion away from Pericles and was beginning to accelerate toward them.

"Alright, Carl, what's going... What is THAT?"

Alison floated up next to him and the Captain, her jaw hanging open as she looked at the lifepod on the camera display. The Captain answered in a matter-of-fact tone.

"ETs, coming to visit."

Alison spluttered in shock.

"Carl, pull up the recording of the ship."

"Aye, Cap'n."

Alison leaned closer to the display as the video from earlier came up on the screen.

"Holy shit," she breathed.

"That's what we thought," replied the Captain. "The main ship just detonated, and that lifepod is on intercept with us. What can we expect from these creatures?"

"How would I know?"

The Captain rested her hands on her hips and gave Alison a stern look.

"You're a doctor. A scientist. Make an educated guess."

Alison frowned in thought for a moment, then shook her head.

"It's hard to know where to start, with no data. Most of the more highly intelligent creatures we've catalogued are bipedal. They would almost certainly have opposable thumbs, if they are able to manufacture tools. Aside from that, who knows?"

The venting gasses in the video recording clicked in Carlton's mind.

"I may be able to help with that, hon. Just a sec."

He stilled the image again and selected the area around the gas cloud, then keyed the spectrographic analyzer. Although the algorithm was optimized to analyze stellar composition and other natural phenomena, absorption and emission lines were the same everywhere. Maybe it could tell them what the venting gasses were.

Sure enough, after the computer chewed on the data for a minute or so, the spectral analysis popped up in a dialogue window.

"Ok, let's see. Looks like Oxygen and Nitrogen, with a fair amount of Helium and Carbon Dioxide."

"That could be engine fuel, or anything else, Carl."

"True, Cap'n, but it's better than nothing. If this is right, looks like about 25% Oxygen, 60% Nitrogen, 5% CO_2, 7% Helium, and the rest trace gasses."

Alison looked at the numbers and pursed her lips.

"That CO_2 concentration would be deadly for us to breathe. No telling if they could adjust to our lower concentration or not. Normal earth atmosphere would be like living at high altitude for them, but…"

"…we keep the O_2 levels lower than normal to reduce the chance of fires," Carlton finished for her. "What effect would breathing 17.5% O_2 have on them?"

"Probably the same as if we were to breathe 13%. Hypoxia."

"So Pericles is a deathtrap for them."

"Yes, but they don't know that," interjected the Captain. "Better to risk possible death than to accept it for certain. Alright, Carl, I'm going to need all hands for this. Sound Action Stations."

"Aye, Cap'n."

He pressed the first of a quartet of buttons on the starboard side of the pilot's station, and the pulsing tones of the ship's General Alarm sounded. Then the three of them made their way off the bridge.

Three

Standard procedure in the event of a general emergency was to muster the crew in the command center. By the time Carlton, Alison, and the Captain arrived, everyone else had gathered, the night shift looking mussed and bleary-eyed.

The Captain strode to the front of the small crowd with a brisk, business-like pace. Turning to face them, she placed her hands on her hips and spoke in a commanding tone.

"All right, people. We've got a situation. Carl, the video please."

Carlton stepped up to the main display screen's control workstation and tapped in a command.

The recording began playing on the screen, to a collective gasp from the crew. Their expressions ranged from awe to excitement to curiosity to fear as the Captain related the events leading up to Carlton sounding the General Alarm.

Malcolm, the Shift Engineer, spoke up in the silence that marked the conclusion of her briefing.

"How do we know it's a lifepod, and not a weapon of some kind?"

The Captain answered, "We don't. But it wouldn't make any sense to attack us, would it?"

"Fair enough. How long until it gets here?"

The Captain looked at Carlton, and he answered.

"It stopped accelerating and is running at .98c. It's 3.5 AU astern, so we have about fifteen and a half hours."

The Captain spoke again.

"We are obligated to render assistance, now that it is possible to do so without stranding ourselves. In the next fifteen hours, we need to figure out how we're going to do that, and then get it done."

There were protests, of course. Several of the crew wanted nothing to do with rescuing unknown aliens who may or may not have as their intention the slaughter of every human aboard so they could claim Pericles as their own. Only the inevitability of being overtaken whether they liked it or not got everyone onboard with the notion.

They set to work.

It was an easy decision to not bring the aliens aboard in section four, if only to keep them as far from the children as possible.

Section 2 contained hydroponics and consumables storage. There, it would be relatively easy, if time-consuming, for Malcolm and his techs to redirect some of the ventilation to raise the oxygen and carbon dioxide levels in a few compartments near the section 2 airlock, so the aliens would have a better chance at adjusting to the atmosphere. It would mean less carbon dioxide going to feed the crops, but in general they received more than they really needed, so it was a relatively safe move.

What to do with the aliens for the duration of the flight was another matter. Alison was hard-pressed to give an opinion as to whether the cryo-suspension units would be usable. They were designed to sustain humans, after all. With no idea as to the aliens' metabolism, there was no telling what the units would do to them. All the same, she was able to modify a few unused units to supply gasses in closer proximity to the concentrations observed from the alien vessel.

That just left figuring out how to ask them to be guinea pigs. With all due respect to his wife and the Captain, Carlton wasn't about to place odds on their chances of accomplishing that.

The final question was how to get the aliens aboard. Carlton and Sven, his night-shift colleague, had that task. They brainstormed several ideas, but were unable to come up with a viable solution until Rachel, the teacher, reminded them of the mooring lights.

Pericles, like every starliner, had a number of moveable, high-powered spotlights mounted in various places on the hull. Their purpose was to aid in mooring, but the crews also put them to good use for other tasks. They were ready made to point the aliens where to go.

Early in the planning process, the Captain ruled out the airlocks in the crew's acceleration quarters or in the shuttle bay - Pericles had one short-range shuttle for commuting back and forth to space stations without full mooring facilities, stored in the same bay where the replacement nav beacons were housed. Getting the aliens from there to a suitable living area would be complex, and the crew would be in a less than optimal defensive posture, should things turn hostile.

That left the rings. Both were equipped with four airlocks, one in each section. Ring A's faced forward, Ring B's faced aft. The logical choice was the airlock to section 2, Ring A.

Preparations took most of the time available, but the key players managed to swap a few hours of sleep before the rendezvous. With a half hour to go, the welcoming commit-tee met in the command center.

The Captain, of course, would take the lead. Sven had re-lieved Carlton as pilot on duty, so Carlton had the job as the Captain's second. Alison would provide medical assistance, if needed. Malcolm insisted on coming along, with Bryce, Stephanie, and James, one of the horticulturists, in case things got ugly.

Carlton was surprised when the Captain agreed to that, and even more surprised when she ordered the small arms locker opened.

All starliners had a small cache of weapons onboard. Nothing special: a dozen slugthrowers and a few plasma rifles. Just enough for basic defense. The odds of ever needing to use them were very small, but there were a num-ber of circumstances that might require it.

Carlton always viewed the weapons the same as a condom: better to have one and not need it, than to need one and not have it. All the same, except to conduct periodic inventories, he had never seen the small arms locker opened.

Carlton gave the Captain a wry grin as he strapped on a slugthrower. "Don't do anything provocative, right Cap'n?"

She sniffed. "Nothing in the procedure about committing suicide." Pulling the straps on her own holster tight, she straightened and looked over the other members of the team. "Everybody ready?"

They all nodded, doing their best to look calm. Bryce wasn't doing so well at acting, Carlton noticed. He licked his lips and adjusted his grip on his plasma rifle every few seconds, and his eyes darted around. He bore watching.

It took a few minutes to get to section 2. Fortunately, each ring had an intra-ring transit system: a small railcar that al-lowed swift transport between the various sections. Without the rail, it would have been a long walk. Nevertheless, by the time they arrived at the airlock, there were only about ten minutes until the lifepod caught up with Pericles.

The airlock was a standard inner and outer door design. To the right of the inner door was a walk-in storage area containing spacesuits and emergency breathing equipment. On the other side, a display screen and control workstation was installed in the wall. Malcolm and Stephanie retrieved breathing equipment from the storage area while the Captain activated the workstation's intercom.

"All set at the airlock. How are our visitors?"

Sven answered promptly, from the command center.

"Five million kilometers astern and closing, Captain. Ready to secure ring rotation at your command."

"Is Janet ready?"

"Yes, ma'am."

"Right. Standby."

The Captain turned away from the console. She took a moment to don a breathing mask and tank, but didn't seal the mask, instead letting it hang loose around her neck.

Her poise impressed Carlton. He was about ready to jump out of his skin, anxious as he felt. But the Captain was in total control. He guessed that's why she got the big bucks.

"I'll order Janet to adjust atmospheres in this section after we're sure there's not going to be trouble. Be at the ready, but don't do anything to provoke them."

With that, she turned back to the workstation and keyed the ship-wide intercom.

"This is the Captain. We're about ten minutes from contact. Prepare for zero-G."

Her voice still echoed down the corridor as she switched back to the command center.

"Sven, secure ring rotation."

"Aye, Captain."

A pause followed while he keyed the command.

"Stopping sequence initiated. Band Brakes applied, thrusters firing. Rings will be secured in eight minutes."

"Very well."

The Captain tapped a few commands on the workstation, and the display screen came to life in two-pane format. The approaching lifepod appeared in one pane, and a high-level ship's status display appeared in the other. Already, the rings were beginning to slow perceptibly on the display. Carlton could feel a small force pushing him toward the far bulkhead as the ring slowed.

The Band Brakes were huge. Carlton had seen one of them removed from the ship's hub during the last maintenance upkeep. Even though he knew intellectually how large it had to be to slow the millions of kilograms of mass contained in each ring, he was nonetheless stunned when he saw it for himself. But large and powerful as they were, the Band Brakes were nowhere near enough to stop the rings all by themselves in any reasonable period of time, just as the Spinning Motors were not powerful enough to get the rings moving by themselves. So the starliners used thrusters, aligned to impart force in-line with or opposed to the rings' direction of rotation, to assist.

Over the next several minutes, the deceleration force remained small, but detectable. It wasn't enough to move an adult standing still, but if you were walking, you might find yourself turned without realizing it. Low mass loose objects and children tended to get pushed though, so procedure required checking all inhabited compartments for stowage and strapping the children in before starting or stopping the rings. More noticeable, the centripetal acceleration from the rings' movement lowered, making everything feel lighter.

Then there was no weight at all. The most minuscule movement pushed Carlton off the floor, and once more he found himself floating in zero-G. His favorite.

Sven's voice piped up over the intercom.

"Ring rotation secured, Captain. Zero-G in all compartments."

"Very well, Sven. Proceed as briefed. Let me know if anything unexpected occurs."

"Aye."

There was nothing to do but wait.

On the display screen, the range to the lifepod ticked down quickly, and its bearing rate began to increase. It looked like the aliens would pass down Pericles' port side. As the range lowered to ten thousand kilometers, the lifepod's forward velocity began lowering rapidly.

Interestingly, the blue-purple glow still appeared from that one location, near the far side of the craft. Carlton had presumed that glow was a thruster of some sort before. But if that were the case, it wouldn't be slowing them now, would it? It was puzzling.

The Captain shifted the other pane from ship's status to one of the hull monitoring cameras. Mounted astern the bridge, facing aft and upward, it provided a good view of the now-motionless rings and the section 2 airlock, stopped at the 2:30 position.

When the lifepod closed within a hundred kilometers, as briefed earlier, Sven shut off Pericles' hull illumination lights. Only the collision avoidance strobes, set at intervals around the rings, and the running lights at the bow and stern remained lit. In the hull monitoring camera, Pericles became a dim object, barely discernible from the interstellar darkness beyond. Then when the lifepod closed to 20 kilometers, Sven turned on four of the powerful spotlights. Two illuminated the lifepod itself, and two illuminated the section 2 airlock outer door.

On the display, the lifepod image completely filled the aft upper camera's field of view, so the Captain shifted to a hull monitoring camera and tracked it in. Much harder to see without the large magnification, it took a couple minutes to find the lifepod as it stopped its relative motion amidships, about five kilometers to port. There it stayed for what seemed an eternity.

In reality, that eternity was just a few minutes. Carlton could imagine the conversation going on aboard the lifepod. "What do they intend?" "Should we go aboard or take our chances in the void?" "Foolish earthlings, don't they know we mean to kill them all and take their women?"

Well, on second thought the alien creatures would probably have no interest whatsoever in human women. But he couldn't rule out hostile intent in his mind, however dire the aliens' circumstances. He found himself reflexively fingering his slugthrower, and thinking maybe Bryce wasn't so far out of line in his jumpiness.

The lifepod turned and began to close Pericles. It quickly closed the kilometers from its holding position and took up position in front of the airlock.

The Captain shifted the camera view to one located not far from the airlock. From that angle, they could see the lifepod rotate in space until one of those circular markings Carlton saw earlier faced the airlock door. The lifepod began moving, ever so slowly, toward the airlock outer door, and everyone took a reflexive step backward.

Except the Captain. She remained at the workstation. As the lifepod drew near, she entered a command, and Carlton could see, through the windows on the inner door, the airlock outer door slide open. He swallowed, trying to loosen the lump in his throat. Glancing around, it looked as though his fellows were doing the same.

A tube extended from the lifepod.

A docking device, no doubt. But it was like no device Carlton had seen, because the end of the tube, where the sealing surface was, morphed in shape as it approached the airlock, until it exactly matched the mating surface on the outer airlock doorframe.

Carlton's jaw dropped as the lifepod made contact and the contact lights on the airlock status display illuminated. How did they do that?

He glanced at Malcolm, and saw he wasn't the only one surprised by this. It wasn't often that Malcolm was impressed, but he wore an awed expression on his face.

The Captain pressed a button on the workstation, and the display shifted to a camera inside the airlock. Carlton heard the hissing sound of rushing air, and the airlock interior pressure indication rose until it reached normal atmospheric, then held steady. One minute later, the pressure hadn't dropped. It was a good seal.

"Sven, positive seal on the airlock. Commence ring rotation."

Sven sounded more than a little on-edge when he responded.

"Aye, Captain. Spin sequence activated. Thrusters firing, Spinning Motors online."

Sven's voice came over the ship-wide intercom, announcing the imminent return of Gs. Then a moment later, ever so slowly, the ring started to move. The mating tunnel flexed a bit, but the seal held, and the lifepod began moving with the ring. The welcoming committee spread out as the closest bulkhead moved toward them. One by one, the team members struck it and pushed themselves down to the deck.

Carlton always found this part amusing. Every so often, a

newbie wouldn't watch himself when rotation started, and would end up getting tangled up with other people. This group was all seasoned, though, so the transition from zero-G to steadily building centripetal acceleration was smooth.

They re-arranged themselves in a semicircle around the airlock inner door, with the Captain a pace ahead of the others. For a few minutes, nothing happened. The gravity slowly built, until they were at about two-thirds earth normal.

Then, on the display, Carlton saw the outer door on the lifepod slide open. This was it.

Four figures emerged from the lifepod. Dressed in loose-fitting grey garments that were not dissimilar to those the humans wore, the aliens were bipedal, as Alison predicted, but they had short tails. They walked barefoot, with a hunch, in quick, fluid steps.

Their gait changed abruptly as they passed from the mating tunnel into the airlock. A step that in the tunnel had barely made their heads bob caused their entire bodies to lift a centimeter or two off the deck.

"Artificial gravity," Malcolm said, echoing Carlton's thoughts. "How do they manage that without spinning, I wonder?"

The quartet paused in the airlock, and the humans got a better look at them on the display.

They were smaller than an average human, but appeared powerfully built. They wore breathing masks, but their facial features were clearly visible. They looked almost feline, with peaked ears atop their heads and elongated snouts. But they were hairless. Their skin was a yellow-orange color, with streaks of green, and it shimmered somewhat as they moved. It took Carlton a minute to figure out the reason: their skin was scaled. Their hands were three-fingered, with opposable thumbs - another point in Alison's favor. Their fingers ended in small points, rather than in pads.

The alien in front removed an instrument of some kind from a pouch on its belt. After studying the instrument for a moment, the alien made a gesture and said something. As it spoke, it revealed razor-sharp teeth and a green, flicking tongue.

All that was fine and dandy, but Carlton zeroed in on one last detail more than the others: they all had what looked like the hilt of a sword sticking up over their right shoulders, and what could only be holsters on their hips.

"Be ready," said the Captain, and she unsnapped the holster on her slugthrower. She noticed the weapons too.

From the corner of his eye, Carlton saw Bryce and Stephanie raise their plasma rifles to their shoulders. They all looked tense. Bryce was sweating up a storm.

The lead alien knocked on the inner door with the instrument it had just used. The sound traveled easily to Carlton's ears. For some reason, it seemed ominous.

"Alison, are you filming?"

Alison had refused the thought of carrying a weapon. She was a doctor, not an undertaker. Instead, she brought along a video recording device. Sven was making recordings of every external and internal camera feed, but few of them had audio, and they didn't cover every area that might be needed, so her recording was going to be the most vital.

"Yes."

"Alright. Malcolm, open the door."

Malcolm stood closest to the control station. He nodded and hit the inner door control switch.

The door opened. There was a slight hiss, and a small breeze, as the pressures between the two spaces equalized. The aliens stepped, one by one, into the room. They looked over the group of humans slowly, then the leader took a step toward the Captain.

"Oh Jesus," Bryce murmured, drawing Carlton's gaze. The guy was shaking badly. Malcolm, the closest to him, looked at Bryce with concern.

Either the Captain didn't hear or it didn't register. She managed a smile and said, "Welcome aboard."

The lead alien cocked it's head to the side. It studied the Captain for a moment after she spoke, then said something that sounded a mix between a hiss and a bark. The leftmost alien reached for its holster.

Bryce shouted, "OH JESUS!" and fired his plasma rifle.

Everything seemed to happen at once.

Four

The Captain screamed, "NO!"

The ball of superheated gas from Bryce's rifle struck the alien in the shoulder, sending it smashing into the bulkhead. It slumped to the ground, clutching at its wound.

The alien's neighbor bounded over to it and crouched down, to render assistance, no doubt.

The leader and the remaining alien turned to see their stricken comrade, for a heartbeat apparently as stunned as Carlton was.

Then they roared, their lips drawing back to reveal their teeth. Turning back to the humans, they seemed to coil as they dropped into low stances and advanced.

Malcolm tackled Bryce, bearing him to the floor and pinning him there. Bryce's rifle went skidding away out of his reach.

Stephanie stood there, a shocked expression on her face.

James fumbled at the snap on his holster.

Carlton found himself doing the same. Why wouldn't the cussed thing unsnap?

"NO!" shouted the Captain again. She jumped in front of the advancing creatures, her hands, empty, raised with palms facing them. "Stop!"

The lead alien grabbed the Captain by the throat and, with one hand, lifted her about twenty centimeters off the deck. It pulled its free hand back as though to punch, but Carlton saw what looked like razor-sharp claws unfolding from the points at the tips of its fingertips.

He got his holster unsnapped and drew his slugthrower. From the corner of his eye, he saw Stephanie sighting in on the leader.

"Don't shoot," the Captain managed to say, her voice sounding strangled.

She waved frantically at them with both hands, forceful downward gestures commanding them to lower their weapons.

Very reluctantly, Carlton complied, and he saw Stephanie do the same. James hadn't gotten his slugthrower out yet.

Malcolm pressed his forearm into the back of Bryce's neck and his knee into Bryce's kidney, drawing exclamations of pain from him.

The alien leader hissed, and its fellow stopped advancing.

The leader looked at the Captain for a long moment, then at Bryce and Malcolm, then at the others. Then, ever so slowly, it lowered the Captain to the ground.

With a bark, it released her and stepped back. The other alien stepped back as well, but its hand found the sword hilt, or whatever the thing was over its shoulder. The alien looked very ready to use it.

The Captain slumped backward, her hand going to her throat. She coughed heavily. Carlton moved forward to support her, but she brushed him aside.

"Alison," the Captain said, her voice still a bit strangled. "Help them."

Nodding, Alison passed the video recorder off to James, and, hefting her medical bag, moved toward the aliens.

She hadn't gone more than two steps before the alien with the sword stepped forward again, growling with menace. She swallowed and opened her bag. Withdrawing a roll of gauze, she held it up for the aliens to see.

The leader made another hiss-bark, in a different tone than the first, and the creature that was tending to their wounded comrade responded in kind.

The medic stood and helped its fellow to its feet. The wounded alien's shoulder was bound with narrow black bands of some material Carlton didn't recognize. It looked like they had first aid under control.

Alison nodded in understanding and backed up, replacing the gauze into her bag.

The leader made another bark, this time with a long, drawn-out hiss at the end. The alien medic led its wounded fellow through the airlock door. The patient gave the humans a look that, had a human made it, promised extreme violence. But it allowed itself to be led out without further incident.

When they left, the leader touched a button on the breast of its uniform. A soft beep sounded, and the leader began speaking, a quick succession of hisses, barks, growls, and whistles. A similar stream of alien words emanated from the button, clearly a communication device of some kind, in response. The leader bobbed its head and waited.

On the camera display, Carlton saw the lifepod's airlock

door open again. Two new aliens stepped into the mating tunnel, pushing a large machine of some sort ahead of them.

The machine hovered in the air. Despite its obvious bulk, it appeared easy to maneuver down the tunnel and into Pericles' airlock. That hovering bit was a neat trick.

The leader moved aside as the new pair pushed the machine through the inner door and into the center of the room. The machine hovered half a meter above the floor, and was about two and a half meters long, a meter wide, and a meter and a half tall. Constructed of black metal, with a transparent hinged lid on top, it had a number of what looked like controls on one end. The lid was frosted over, making it difficult to see inside.

After they finished positioning the machine, the two new aliens turned and went back to the lifepod.

The leader stepped up to the machine and ran a hand over the lid. It was almost a caress.

The strangely tender moment ended quickly. The leader straightened and turned to the Captain. It made another sound, a cross between a hiss and a growl, and gestured for her to approach.

The Captain nodded and, swallowing, stepped forward. Carlton noticed she was being very careful to keep her hands empty and plainly in view. That didn't seem such a bad policy, considering.

The leader moved over to the machine's control panel and gestured again for the Captain to follow. When she reached its side, it pointed to a button on the panel and looked back at her. She nodded, and the leader touched the button. A low-frequency tone sounded, and the machine slowly lowered to the floor. The leader pressed the button again, and a higher frequency tone sounded. The machine rose from the floor and after a moment was hovering once more.

The leader lowered the machine back to the floor then moved to the next button. But before pushing it, the leader made a chopping motion with its free hand and issued another bark-hiss phrase. From the way it sounded out the words, whatever they were, Carlton surmised whatever the leader said was very important.

The leader pressed the second button, and the lid cracked open. Clouds of steam poured through the crack. Carlton checked himself. That wasn't steam; it sank to the floor after it escaped the machine. It reminded him of melting dry ice.

The leader pushed the lid fully open and reached inside the machine. It withdrew an oval object, a bit larger than a baseball. It was green, streaked with yellow. It had a wrinkled, leathery texture, but appeared firm in the alien's grasp.

The leader turned back to the Captain and looked at her. Cradling the object in its arm, the leader gently pet it. Then, looking the Captain in the eyes, the leader pressed its free hand to its belly, then to the object.

"An egg," Alison said softly.

Stephanie gasped, and the Captain's eyes widened as the truth of Alison's analysis hit home.

The leader, apparently satisfied at their reactions, replaced the egg in the machine and pressed the second button. The lid shut with a solid click, and almost immediately frosted over again.

Turning back to the Captain, the leader then withdrew a rectangular black object from behind its belt. The object was about eight centimeters long, two and a half wide, and one centimeter deep. There were three raised red areas on it. The leader pointed to the first red area, and touched it.

In the space above the object, a three dimensional image appeared. The image was clearly holographic, an impressive enough feat that for a moment it distracted Carlton from what he was actually looking at: a star chart. In the lower portion of the image, a flashing green dot was visible, as well as a curved yellow line leading from the dot to a small star. Carlton knew his star charts well enough to recognize the green dot as their current location, and the small star as Sol. The aliens must have plotted out Pericles' course to determine their destination. It wouldn't be that hard to do.

The leader moved its finger into the image of Sol, and a new line, this one blue, appeared, leading from Sol across the chart to another, larger, star system. From what Carlton could tell of the scale, the second system was at least two hundred light years from Sol, well outside the area mankind had explored. The leader pointed at the Captain, then laid its hand on the machine. Finally, it pointed to the star system at the end of the blue line.

That couldn't mean what Carlton thought it meant, could it?

The Captain seemed to be having similar thoughts.

"Sir, we can't…"

The leader cut her off with a mixture growl and whistle. Then, again, it pointed from her to the machine to the star.

The Captain sighed and nodded.

The leader growled quickly, then pressed the second red area on the object.

The star chart disappeared, replaced by an image of the leader. It began speaking, more of the same grunts, growls, barks, and the rest. The speech cut off as the leader pressed the first red area again, and the star chart re-appaeared. It pointed at the second red area, then at the star at the end of the blue line.

The Captain nodded again, and the leader pressed the final red area.

One dot appeared, with a strange symbol next to it. A second later, that was replaced by two dots, with a different symbol. Then three, then four, all the way up to eight. Then different combinations of the symbols appeared, along with others. The image continued on like that for a minute or so, and then shifted to become a continuous sequence of symbols, probably a hundred fifty characters across and a hundred lines in length. The leader whistled, and waved its hand above the red area. The image shifted to another sequence, different from the first. Then, with another wave, yet another sequence appeared. What the hell was that supposed to be?

The Captain looked baffled also, but Malcolm's eyebrows had risen high onto his forehead. He wore an expression of awe. Catching Carlton's gaze, he spoke softly.

"It's their mathematics."

Carlton frowned. Why was that so impressive? Then it hit him. With knowledge of the aliens' mathematics, humans could translate scientific formulas, or technical specifications. Carlton would bet good money that's what those final pages of symbols were.

The leader pressed the third red area again, and the image disappeared. It pointed at the red area, then pointed at the Captain and the rest of the team in turn, even Bryce. Finally, with a low growl, followed by a bark, it held the rectangular object out toward the Captain.

Slowly, gingerly, she reached out and took it.

The leader made a hiss-bark similar to one it made earlier, and its companion backed away into the airlock. When it had gone, the leader made a strangely intricate gesture with its hands, ending with an inclination of its head toward the Captain. Then, it turned and strode out of the room, into the airlock.

"Where's he going?" Carlton asked.

The entire welcoming committee moved to the inner airlock door, all save Bryce, who remained lying on the floor, despite Malcolm releasing him from the submission hold.

The alien leader didn't look back, but walked straight into the lifepod's airlock. The door shut quickly behind it.

They all looked at each other in confusion, and no small amount of shock. Then lights began flashing in the mating tunnel, and a oscillating siren sounded. Malcolm's eyes widened, and he quickly moved to the airlock control console. He hit a button, and the outer airlock doors slid shut.

No sooner had they done so than the mating tunnel detached. Through the small window in the outer airlock doors, they saw the tunnel begin to retract, then it and the lifepod disappeared, leaving nothing visible but the slowly rotating starfield.

The Captain rushed to the workstation and called up the external camera view. Nothing. She hit the intercom to the command center.

"Sven! Where did it go?"

Sven, sounding nearly breathless, responded promptly.

"Just off the starboard side, Captain, moving away at about seventy meters per second. Wait. Velocity is increasing rapidly. Gained visual on the number 6 hull monitoring camera."

"Right." She called up that camera, and they all saw the lifepod moving quickly away. Very soon it was too far away to make out without additional magnification, and she shifted to the forward upper camera, which Sven directed to track the lifepod.

Malcolm hit the control for the inner door, and it slid shut. Then he spoke.

"It makes sense, Captain. They would have continued on

in the same direction as the velocity vector they had the instant before they detached. On the first deck, the rings rotate at about seventy meters per second, so…"

The Captain interrupted him.

"I understand physics, Malcolm. Why the hell did they leave?"

Bryce, still lying there with his face pressed to the floor, sobbed.

"I'm sorry, Captain. I was so scared. I thought it was pulling a gun."

The Captain gave him a withering look. Good thing for him he couldn't see it, or he'd either turn to stone or burst into flame. Then her expression softened. Carlton was surprised by that, but not by her reply.

"It's alright, Bryce. We were all scared. I shouldn't have put you in that position."

Bryce looked up, a grateful expression on his face. Then, wiping his nose, he sat up. Probably he didn't get the deeper meaning to her statement. Carlton was sure Bryce would never see high-stress tasking again. He did not know it, but his career just came to a standstill, at least on this ship.

Carlton cleared his throat.

"Am I crazy, or did they just ask us to…"

He stopped speaking as a bright flash on the display drew his, and everyone else's, attention. His eyes went wide as he realized what he was seeing. Where the lifepod used to be, there was only an expanding cloud of hot gasses and shrapnel.

The Captain hit the intercom again.

"Sven! How far was it when it blew?"

"Five hundred kilometers, Captain. I'm tracking the largest fragments. They should pass well clear of us."

The Captain let out a breath, her expression one of relief.

"Very well."

She switched to the ship-wide intercom.

"Attention, this is the Captain. Our visitors have departed. Resume normal watch routine. That is all."

With that, she turned back to the group. Nodding to Carlton, she spoke again.

"Yes, Carl, they did. They want us to deliver their eggs to their homeworld."

From her tone of voice, she was just as confused as he felt. Malcolm spoke up.

"Probably that reading they took in the airlock is what did it, Captain." He held up a hand to forestall a retort. "They got data on our atmosphere as soon as they entered the tunnel. When they got to the airlock, they also got data on our gravitation. They probably realized they couldn't survive on our ship for long, and went with plan B. The eggs are on ice. Don't need the same resources they do. So at least they have a chance to preserve something of themselves. Assuming we keep our end of the deal."

"Why should we?" James asked. "We've got enough to worry about."

"They paid us, for one thing," Malcolm retorted.

"And it's the right thing to do," the Captain added. She looked at the alien machine, with its precious cargo, and sighed. "Let's get this thing stowed. Malcolm, figure out what kind of power it needs and rig up something to provide it."

Malcolm looked askance at her and opened his mouth to reply, but stopped after a second and nodded, saying nothing.

The Captain traced her fingers along the length of the artifact and pursed her lips. "Carl, we're going to have one hell of a message to send. Get a draft ready for review by the end of this watch. For the rest of you," she looked at each crewmember in turn, "as far as anyone off this ship knows, this never happened. No talking about it except for what is necessary for shift turnover."

"You're not really thinking of changing course?" James sounded incredulous, but also afraid.

The Captain shook her head, shooting him a withering look. "Of course not. We don't have the fuel for that sort of adjustment. And besides, we've got passengers and cargo who need to get to Earth. When we get there, we'll turn this thing over to the authorities, and they will see it sent home."

"So much for the boring center passage," Carlton said, trying to insert a bit of humor.

The Captain looked at him, but her expression was one of resignation. She shook her head and sighed again. "Space travel sucks sometimes, doesn't it?"

So You Want To Be
A Dragon Slayer...

D

o you want to be a Dragon Slayer?"

The advertisement was only a fifteen second spot in a late night time slot. I wouldn't have paid any attention to it at all, but that catch phrase caught my attention and called to the part of me that used to play role playing games when I was a kid. I gave up on that sort of thing a long time ago, replacing imagination with practicality as I settled into adult life. But part of me wished that those games I'd played back in the day could be true. So when I heard that phrase, with a catchy jingle behind it, I got sucked in.

I had to see what that advertisement was all about.

The corporate offices of Dragon Safaris, Inc resided in a small building near the edge of downtown, close enough to the big money companies to bask in their glow but far enough out that the rent was probably almost reasonable. I convinced Vinnie and Carl, my last two buds from high school, to come with me. All the other members of our old crew had shipped off to other places: Johnny to the Marines, Dave to work in the fuel refineries on Titan, and Steve... Well, Steve was still in town, but none of us knew where. Or cared to. Word was, he'd fallen in with a bad crowd and taken up drug smuggling or something. Poor guy.

The three of us paused in front of the office doors. Despite my curiosity, my eagerness really, I felt hesitant to enter. What if it was just another stupid scam: some second-rate animatronics or something? I'd feel like a real ass bringing my friends along for something like that. I almost turned and walked away.

But then I heard the jingle in my head again, along with that phrase. And I found myself saying, silently, "Yes, I do want to be a Dragon Slayer."

I walked inside before the thought finished going through my head.

At first, I was underwhelmed. The reception area was nothing special. I'd been in dozens of places just like it. Granted, none of those other businesses had a logo as cool as the one Dragon Safaris had suspended behind the receptionist's desk, but that was hardly a surprise. How cool could a doctor's logo be without scaring off the patients?

The receptionist perked up as we walked in and offered us a standard issue customer service smile. "Good afternoon. Welcome to Dragon Safaris," she said. "Do you have an appointment?"

I shook my head. "Didn't know we needed one."

She opened her mouth to reply, but I continued quickly before she could tell us to leave.

"We just have some questions about how this works. Do

you have any documentation, or…"

The receptionist sniffed. "I was just going to say we have a presentation that covers frequently asked questions. Through the first door on the left." She gestured down the hall, which departed the reception area to her right.

I glanced at Vinnie and Carl. They both shrugged acquiescence, so we headed down the hallway.

The presentation room was small, set up like a theater with several lounge chairs facing a screen on the far wall. As we sat down, the lights dimmed and a video production started.

First was a star field with a deep male voiceover.

"For centuries, mankind has told legends of the dragon. Powerful. Majestic. Mystical. The dragon was revered, worshipped, feared."

The star field shifted, zooming in on a single star system.

"Legends tell of brave men who risked everything and battled the dragon to protect the helpless from its ravishing."

A brilliant white star filled the display screen. Several smaller orbs revolved around it in clockwise orbits. The display tracked in on one of the planets in particular, the fifth in the system. It quickly grew in the picture until it dominated the display. Blue-green in color, with swirling clouds covering most of its surface, it was beautiful to look at.

The picture zoomed in further.

"Other men throughout the ages longed to test themselves against these creatures of legend, but were unable to reach into myth to do so."

Clouds rushed past as the camera descended into the planet's atmosphere. I noticed the lack of re-entry plasma and sniffed. They could have at least gotten that right. The voiceover spoke again.

"Until now."

The clouds parted, and a ear-shattering roar came through

over the speakers. A huge creature with webbed wings and a long, serpentine neck flew overhead, then dove through the camera's view toward the ground. Rolling and pitching downward to follow the creature, the image on the display tracked its descent toward a mountain peak far below.

"Reptus Volans, the great flying beasts of Alcor Five, render that world too dangerous to colonize."

The beast landed atop the peak and, looking back up at the camera, roared again, revealing a mouth filled with long, sharp teeth.

"But where the Colonial Allocation Committee saw failure, we at Dragon Safaris see opportunity."

The screen changed, depicting a clean, laboratory-like room with a large metal ring mounted perpendicular to the center of the floor. Parts of the ring lit up, and a vortex began to form in the center of the ring. The vortex grew larger and larger until it filled the ring completely. Then there was a brilliant flash of light. When the light faded, wooded terrain, clearly a different place than the room, could be seen through the ring.

"Using state of the art space portal technology, Dragon Safari engineers can have you on Alcor Five faster than you ever thought possible. There, skilled guides will lead you on a journey of legendary proportions as you track down and challenge a dragon in a fight to the death."

A new image came up on the screen. It showed a group of grinning men, all dressed in some kind of armor plating and carrying fancy-looking rifles, posing before a dead beast that was obviously the same species as the one from earlier in the video.

"Dragon Safaris has a full selection of weapons and protective gear designed specifically for this adventure."

A panning video moved through what was clearly an armory. Breastplates, helmets, leg and arm protectors, and gauntlets hung from racks. Then the video moved through a doorway into another room. Every corner of the room held a weapon of some sort.

"The modern hunter has his choice of top-shelf projectile or plasma weapons. But for the more...adventurous customer, we have a more classical selection."

The video moved through another doorway. The next room was lined with bows, spears, swords, and axes. My jaw fell open.

"Are you ready?"

The video returned to the earlier clip of the beast sitting atop the peak, roaring.

"Are you worthy?"

The screen went black and the lights came back up. I have to admit, I was stunned. Oh, I'd heard that Alcor Five wasn't to be colonized because of dangerous wildlife. But I'd never heard anything more specific. Or seen any pictures of the creatures. It was amazing! Those things could have been transported directly out of the old swords and sorcery stories or out of my role playing games.

I had to do this.

"Oh, hell yeah," Vinnie said. I turned to look at him and returned his ear-to-ear grin with one of my own.

The earliest appointment we could get was a week later. That week seemed to drag. Every day at work, I was distracted by thoughts of the adventure ahead. Every night, I broke out my old role playing game rule books, which I'd long ago stashed away in a box in my basement. I spent hours reading and re-reading them. When the week was finally over and we met back up at the Dragon Safaris offices, I was practically bursting at the seems with excitement.

We were met in the reception area by a chubby, balding guy

in his late 30s or early 40s. He introduced himself as Stanley Jergesen then led us back to his office, a bit further down the hallway past the presentation room and through an imposing set of double doors that Stanley had to unlock using an electronic cypher. His office was plain; just a desk, a file cabinet, and a few chairs for us to sit in. He offered us something to drink. I declined. Carl, however, eagerly accepted a cup of Joe.

"So, gentlemen," Stanley said, getting down to business. "You're interested in taking a little trip, hmm?" His eyebrows rose on his forehead and his lips curled upward in an inviting grin.

We all nodded.

"Excellent." Stanley tapped his desk, and an area of the wall to his left flashed to life with the company logo. "Would you like the modern package or the classical?"

"Classical," I said immediately.

"Definitely classical," agreed Vinnie.

Carl shrugged.

Stanley's grin almost turned into a smirk for a second, but quickly returned to normal. Nodding, he tapped the desktop a few times, and the display shifted to show the collection of old-fashioned weapons from the presentation video. "Now then, have any of you ever used a sword or bow before?"

"You mean besides in Dungeons and Dragons?" Carl quipped.

Stanley really did smirk this time. "Yes, besides that."

We all shook our heads.

With a sigh, Stanley said, "In that case, may I suggest you go with the modern package? Those weapons are far easier to learn to use properly, and…"

I cut him off. "Classical, Stanley."

He sighed again. "Very well." With that, he turned around

in his chair to the file cabinet and opened one of the drawers. He took a moment to rifle through a few folders, then turned back around and slid a piece of paper across his desk toward each of us, along with a pen. "This is a standard waiver of liability and insurance form. Part of your fee will cover medical treatment for injuries sustained during the expedition, but you agree to hold Dragon Safaris blameless for any permanent disability or death that may happen as a consequence of your participation."

I immediately stiffened, feeling put off by the entire concept. But after a moment's thought, I realized it made sense. These dragon things were pretty big, and the trip would probably be dangerous. The liability insurance premiums alone would make it impossible for Dragon Safaris to stay in business if they didn't have some sort of waiver in place. Heck, I remembered having to sign a waiver before riding on a roller coaster once. How was this any different?

I signed the waiver and slid it back to him. He nodded to me, then to Carl and Vinnie in turn as he accepted their signed papers also.

"Now that that's out of the way," Stanley said, his grin returning easily to his face, "we can get down to business. Your package consists of a medical evaluation followed by two weeks of preparation and weapons training, then a two-day journey to Alcor Five. Our guides will do their best to find a dragon for you, but we cannot guarantee..."

"Cannot guarantee? You've got to be kidding me," Carl said. "What the hell are we paying you for then?"

Stanley's smile slipped. "Your down payment will cover the cost of your training and the trip itself. The hunting fee is payable upon completion of your trip, assuming you find a dragon. If you do not, you owe nothing more." He drew a breath, then added, "I would add, however, that the reason the CAC disapproved Alcor Five for colonization is the planet's large Reptus population. We have yet to send an expedition that did not encounter one."

"What if it gets away before we kill it?" Vinnie inquired. My thoughts exactly.

Stanley spread his hands in a helpless gesture. "We can only promise the opportunity, sir."

Vinnie nodded slowly, not looking pleased with that answer.

Stanley was silent for a moment as though he expected another question. Then, shrugging, he tapped his desktop again, and the display shifted. "Here is the cost breakdown for the classical package. As you can see, the total cost…"

"…Is fricking ridiculous!" Carl said.

Stanley looked at him with a bemused expression. "We are not only training you for two weeks, providing you with room and board for that time and a pair of highly skilled guides for your journey, but we're sending you to another world 82 light years away. Those expenses add up quickly."

Carl withered a little bit as Stanley's logic sank in.

"Is that the total cost, or the cost for each of us?" I asked, gesturing toward the calculations on the display screen

"Total," Stanley replied, and I, at least, relaxed a bit. Carl was right: it was a lot of money. But split three ways, it would be quite a bit easier to come up with.

"Don't worry, Carl, Vinnie and I can help you out," I offered, preparing myself for the inevitable pushback. Carl was a proud guy, but he didn't make much money. And he hated when someone else mentioned that fact, or even alluded to it.

I was surprised, though, because he didn't fire back. He just nodded and said, "Thanks, bro." He must have been as excited to do this as I was, though as usual it was impossible to tell from looking at him.

In reality, Vinnie was the money bags of our little group. His accounting business had been on fire lately, and he was really raking it in. He wouldn't tell us how much he earned these days, but it was obviously a lot; his house was paid off and he had a great car, a sailboat in a slip on the lake, and lots of designer clothes. Not that I was doing badly by any stretch of the imagination. But he was definitely top dog among us, at least financially. So really there was never a concern about being able to afford this trip, but we had an unspoken rule: no mooching. Everyone chips in his fair share. It had served us well over the years, and we were not about to cast that rule aside.

And so we all ponied up as much as we could. Vinnie paid the lion's share, I covered most of the rest, and Carl finished it off. I could tell he was unhappy, both from being able to contribute so little and from parting with that much cash all at once. But he didn't say anything. All of a sudden, I was very proud to be his friend.

Stanley's smile was quite a bit broader once we'd signed all the other papers and transferred the funds for the down payment. Rubbing his hands together, almost with glee it appeared, he tapped his desktop control pad again and a calendar appeared on the wall display. "Alright. Let's see," he said as he paged through the weeks. "The next opening is in…two months." He looked from the wall display to us.

"Two months!" Vinnie exclaimed. "You're kidding!"

Stanley shrugged apologetically. "I'm sorry sir, but as you can see there is a large demand for our services, and it is growing every day. This time next year, you'll be lucky to be able to book a year out."

"A lot can happen in two months, Stan," I said, also frowning. "That's a lot of money."

"Ah," he replied. "No need to worry about that, gentlemen. Your down payment is completely refundable up until three days before your training starts. No questions asked."

That seemed fair enough.

If waiting a week for the first appointment was difficult, waiting two months to actually get started was nearly torture. But eventually the time passed and we all met up again, ready to get to it. Stanley met us in the reception area and once more led us through the locked double doors. But this time, we went past his office, through several more twists and turns of the corridor, and finally into a larger room that was set up as a dormitory. A half-dozen beds were spaced evenly along one wall, with lockers on the other wall opposite each bed. Two fit looking people, a flaxen-haired woman and a dark-complected man, were waiting for us.

"Gentlemen, meet your instructors and guides during your adventure," Stanley said. "Johan is a master of wilderness survival. He's worked with special forces and has led hunting expeditions of all varieties. Kimberly's training is in endurance events and the martial arts." There was a long silence, and I could feel both sets of eyes scanning us, judging every little detail as Stanley made the introductions. It was not a comfortable feeling. Then Stanley cleared his throat, drawing every eye to himself. "Right. I'll leave you in their capable hands. Best of luck, gentlemen."

With that, Stanley smiled and left us.

"Pick a rack," Johan said in a deep baritone. "You've got thirty minutes to get settled in, then we'll begin your training." Then he and Kimberly also left.

Vinnie whistled softly as the door slid shut behind them. "Oh man, I just found the only rack I want to rest my head on. Did you see her?"

Carl snorted. "Whatever. She's a butterface."

Vinnie looked at him, a perplexed expression on his face. "Huh?"

I couldn't help but chuckle. "Jesus, Vinnie. You know: nice body, but her face!"

"Yeah, you might have to brown bag it if you hooked up with her," Carl added, gesturing as though he was putting on a hat that covered his entire head.

We both laughed.

Vinnie flushed and grumbled something under his breath, then set about unpacking.

True to their word, Kimberly and Johan returned after a half hour. To the second. They only paused in the dormitory long enough to look us over and gesture for us to follow before they turned and walked away.

The first stop was the medical exam. Three men in white lab coats waited for us in an exam room that was the same as every other one I'd ever been in except that it had five beds separated by sliding curtains. For an hour, they ran the standard battery of tests: height, weight, blood pressure, blood work, reflexes, hernia, eyes and ears. The usual. By the end of the hour, I was about ready to ask for a refund.

Then Johan and Kimberly returned and the Docs released us to their custody again. They led us around a few more corners and through a wide set of double doors into the armory. Things were looking up.

Just as in the video presentation, the armory was filled with protective gear for every part of the body. Up close, though, it wasn't quite as impressive as it had been on camera. When Johan prompted us to try on a breastplate, I immediately hefted one. It maybe weighed two kilograms tops and it looked like something I could break over my knee with ease. That wouldn't do at all.

"Really, dude? Plastic?" I flicked the edge of the breastplate with my fingertip as I said that, and was less than impressed at the insignificant little tapping sound that it made.

I wasn't prepared for Kimberly's snort.

"That's not plastic," she said as she snatched the breastplate out of my hands. Without another word, she placed it on a mannequin that stood in the center of the room. Then she went into the next room. She returned a few seconds later with a pistol, which she pointed at the breastplate and fired. The plasma ball from the pistol impacted the breastplate and exploded into a larger burst of flame and heat. When it cleared, the breastplate was still on the mannequin, intact. The only sign that Kimberly had fired was a small scorch mark in the center of the armor piece.

"Whoa."

She smirked. "Whoa is right. This is high-tensile composite material, the same stuff the Marines use for the armor plating on their assault vehicles. It'll take a hell of a beating so you don't have to."

"If the dragon shoots a plasma pistol at us," Carl said.

Kimberly eyed him appraisingly for a moment before answering. "It's also effective against punctures. It's not as good at protecting against blunt force trauma, though, for obvious reasons."

With that, she looked at Johan with a raised eyebrow. He nodded and looked from Carl to Vinnie and then me. "Any other questions gentlemen?" he asked. When no one said anything he clapped his hands together and grinned. "Alright, let's get you suited up."

The armor was easier to put on than I thought it would be. Parts of it really weren't all that much different from my football pads back in High School. The hardest part was getting measured properly and finding the right size parts, but once that was done I was fully dressed in just a few minutes.

I was surprised to find it was also easier to move around in than I first envisioned. The armor was snug, but relatively light-weight. To test it out, I ran in place for a minute, then did some jumping jacks and lunges. The armor hardly interfered with my movement at all. Truth be told, it was almost as easy to move around in as jeans and a t-shirt. Almost.

Vinnie and Carl were waiting when I returned from getting dressed out. They looked completely different in their armor: more rugged, stronger. Maybe it was just the way they carried themselves. Carl tended to slouch normally, but in his armor he stood straight and tall. Vinnie's normally joking grin was less pronounced, more serious. It was as though, once donning the armor, they had begun settling into the hero's role. From their reactions to my entrance, I supposed maybe I had done the same. Just like old times around the gaming table.

Johan looked us over, carefully checking the various straps on the armor pieces. Finally, as I was beginning to feel uncomfortable, he straightened and nodded. "Ok, let's get to work." He made a small gesture to Kimberly and she led us through another doorway on the far end of the armory.

Just as in the video, the two weapons storage areas were large and filled to bursting with all manner of violent tools. Kimberly led us swiftly through the first room, not bothering to point out the selection of firearms. As we walked through, I thought for a moment that perhaps Stanley had been right. Maybe we should take some rifles. It sure would be...

Then I stepped into the second room and lost track of that thought.

The classical weapons room brought an instant grin to my face. Swords hung from racks on the wall to my right.

Spears were mounted in front of me. Axes were caddy-corner to the swords, and bows were opposite them. I rubbed my hands together in anticipation. This is what I'd always fantasized about during all those gaming sessions. Screw that rifle bit. If I was going to kill a dragon, I was going to do it with a sword and spear.

Of course, it was easy to say that. But over the next two weeks, we all learned just how difficult accomplishing that goal was going to be.

The rest of that day and the entirety of the first week was devoted almost exclusively to learning the weapons. Each morning, Johan and Kimberly woke us at 5 am for an hour of calisthenics. Then, after a half hour of breakfast, Kimberly led us through two hours with the sword followed by another two with the axe. We broke for an hour and a half lunch, then Kimberly got us going again with sessions on the spear and bow. Around 5 pm, we had dinner. Then in the evening, we got to spar.

At first, sparring seemed silly to me. After all, Dragons can't use swords and spears so it wasn't like we were going to get into a duel with someone. But by the third day, I began to understand that sparring sharpened the lessons Kimberly taught us. It was one thing to listen to her, or to shadowbox against a target dummy. It was another thing to react to a real person's moves and try to counter with my own.

Obviously, a week of training, no matter how intense, is hardly sufficient to make anyone proficient. The best I could say was by the end of the week, I wasn't in any danger of stabbing myself by accident. And I realized, to my surprise, that I vastly preferred the axe to the sword. It was simpler, more straightforward.

See thing. Hit thing. Hard.

It was the same with the spear. I could throw one of those

a good distance, and stab with it. But shooting a bow? I snapped the bowstring against my forearm more often than not. I was glad to put the bow down at the end of each session.

Carl, on the other hand, seemed to really love the sword. One blade in particular, lighter than the broadswords I'd tried to use, appealed to him. In our sparring sessions, he literally danced circles around me, flicking me with that thing twice for each swing I tried to take at him.

Vinnie had trouble with the melee weapons, but he took to the bow naturally. By day five, he was hitting the target fairly consistently.

He had a lot less luck hitting on Kimberly, though. Vinnie tried his best, using all the good lines that worked so well in the bars. But all he ever got from her was a thorough beating in the sparring ring. Much as I loved him, though, I had to admit that Vinnie was never good at taking a hint. So he kept on trying despite the fact that Kimberly was visibly becoming more annoyed each day. Finally, Johan pulled him aside on the morning of the fourth day. I didn't hear the conversation. But whatever Johan said, Vinnie returned to the group looking positively chastened and never tried to hit on Kimberly again. He immediately got a lot better with the weapons though.

Vinnie's romantic failures aside, it's safe to say that by the end of that week, we were all feeling a little bit cocky. Or at least we acted like it. Not so deep down, I thanked the Lord that there was no possibility of getting into a real melee with any people, because we'd get our butts kicked. All the same, I felt good, like I'd accomplished something, and I found myself walking back to the dorm with a bit of my old varsity football swagger. I couldn't remember the last time I'd walked that way.

Johan took over the lead spot again as we began the second training week. Kimberly still led weapons training sessions in the evenings, but the days were filled with lectures. Alcor Five's geography, weather patterns, known Reptus nesting sites, Reptus anatomy, our planned arrival coordinates, basic first aid, basic wilderness survival, emergency procedures, Johan covered it all. It was a lot to absorb in a short time.

Before I realized it, the second week was over. It was time.

The evening before we departed, Johan showed us one last presentation. There was no well-produced video stream like in the sales presentation. No slides filled with data or descriptions of some thing or other. It was just a series of images that streamed slowly across the display. Each image showed a man, or sometimes a woman, who suffered from varying degrees of injury until, near the end of the photo stream, it was obvious the person in the picture was dead.

I swallowed to keep from getting sick as the pictures became more and more gruesome. Next to me, Vinnie squirmed in his seat; he looked a bit green himself. Carl was stoic, as usual.

Johan cleared his throat, and I was happy to turn my attention away from the pictures and onto him.

"Dragon Safaris has been in business for two and a half years. In that time, over five hundred sportsmen and adventurers have hunted the Reptus. Thirty-five received serious injuries that required hospitalization once they returned. Four died." He paused for effect, looking each of us in the eye for a moment. "They died because they didn't heed their training and because they didn't listen to their guides on the trip. They tried to hot dog it, and paid the price. The Reptus is a powerful beast, and it can kill you in a second, armor or no, if you don't respect it."

Kimberly walked over to a small cabinet against the wall opposite the door and pulled out three spiral-bound booklets. She handed one to each of us and said, "This is a full description of the medical policy associated with your trip. It also has space for you to write down emergency contact data for your next of kin, should anything happen to you. In the back is a pre-prepared template for a Last Will and Testament. We only require the contact information, but I would highly encourage you to make out a will if you haven't already. An attorney and notary will be available in the morning before we leave to officially register the will, if you wish."

"Are there any last questions?" asked Johan.

I had a million questions, but none that really pertained to the immediate situation at hand. I shook my head no.

Johan nodded. "That's it, then. Get a good night's sleep. Tomorrow and the day after will be very taxing, so you'd better charge up your batteries while you can."

That was easy for him to say.

Back in the dorm, we read through the medical policy. It was surprisingly comprehensive, actually. I guess Dragon Safaris didn't want to leave itself open to any medical liability. Then, after filling out the contact data and naming each other as beneficiaries in our respective wills, we hit the sack.

Anxiety kept me awake for a long time that night. I lay there, staring at the ceiling, and suddenly began second guessing the entire venture. What the hell was I thinking? I was going to travel 82 light years to pick a fight with a flying lizard the size of a bus? Had I lost my senses completely? I found myself trembling, and had to suppress a sudden urge to get up out of bed and run home, and to hell with the whole thing.

But then I looked over at my buddies in their beds and

found them both lying awake the same as I was.

"Dude, we've got to be freaking crazy," Vinnie said into the silence.

I burst out laughing, and kept on laughing until I fell asleep.

The next morning, bright and early, we suited up into our armor and selected our weapons. I selected an axe and four throwing spears that were designed to collapse down into a harness on my back. Carl equipped himself the same, except that he took a sword. Vinnie took a bow and a long-bladed knife.

As we filed out of the armory and down the corridor to the transport room, Kimberly waved a device of some sort over our spear tips and arrow heads.

"What are you doing?" I asked.

"The missile weapons all have explosive charges in their tips to give them a bit more punch," she replied. "This device activates them."

"Can they go off?" Carl asked, suddenly looking worried.

She shook her head. "Final arming occurs in flight. It runs off an accelerometer in the spear or arrow itself. Even if you dropped it onto its tip, that wouldn't be enough to set off the charge."

That made me feel a little bit better, but it sure would have been nice to learn about that little feature earlier.

For their part, Johan and Kimberly weren't going the classical route. They each had a plasma rifle slung over their shoulders and pistols on their hips along with knives similar to Vinnie's. The plan was for them to not get involved in the actual fight with the Reptus unless absolutely necessary, as a last resort if it all went to hell. Given that, I supposed it made sense for them to pack as much firepower as possible.

The transport room was the same sterile, laboratory-looking room from the information video. The portal itself was deceptively simple-looking. Eight feet across, it looked like a plain metal hoop with some inset lighting. Of course, appearances can be deceptive, and that was doubly true in this case. During our two month wait, I'd done a bit of research on space portal technology. That thin ring was about to direct hundreds of millions of kilojoules of energy and create an Einstein-Rosen bridge. Un-freaking-believable.

A control station was mounted on the wall near the doorway. A technician in a light-blue jumpsuit with the Dragon Safaris logo on the breast punched in a few commands and the lights in the portal lit up. Just as in the video, a vortex slowly began to form in the center of the ring. Gradually the vortex grew larger until it filled the ring. Then, right on cue, came the flash of light.

It took a moment to blink away the purplish spots from my eyes. I cursed myself for a fool the entire while; I had known that flash was coming, after all.

Finally, my vision cleared enough to see through the ring. It opened onto a field atop a hill that overlooked rolling terrain. The sky was pinkish blue, and mottled with puffy white clouds. A wind was blowing; I could tell from the way the long leaves in a nearby copse of trees swayed. But not even a hint of breeze came through into the transport room.

I looked at the technician. No doubt he could see the quizzical expression on my face, as he chuckled and said, "The portal sets up a semi-permeable boundary with the destination planet. Only items with a field that matches the portal can pass through." He pointed at the Dragon Safaris logo on each piece of armor we wore, and on each of our weapons. The dragon's eyes in the logos had begun glowing red. "As long as you've got one of those still working, you'll be able to get back."

"That's good to know," I said a bit breathlessly.

"Right," said Johan, clapping his hands together. "Let's move out. Remember, stay close to Kimberly and me."

With that, he stepped through the portal. He seemed to elongate for a second, then he was through, looking the same as he always did. Kimberly followed right on his heels, and experienced the same effect.

Carl, Vinnie, and I exchanged long looks. I swallowed, even though I didn't really need to since my mouth was suddenly dry. I hoped I didn't look as nervous as I felt. Vinnie and Carl sure managed to maintain a calm demeanor.

"Well, here goes nothing," Carl said, and he stepped through the portal.

Vinnie went next.

I brought up the rear.

Arriving on Alcor Five was a shock. The air was hot, thick, very sticky, and filled with unfamiliar scents. The ground was spongy, almost like walking on astroturf, and I immediately felt lighter. That made sense considering Alcor Five only had about eighty-five percent of normal earth gravity. But it's one thing to expect something intellectually and another to experience it first hand. I'd never been off world before. Up until this point, a thing weighed what it weighed, no matter what the science textbooks said. No longer.

Johan wasted no time. He immediately turned west and set off down the hill. Supposedly there was a Reptus nest somewhere over in that direction. We all fell in behind him; first Vinnie, then Carl, me, and finally Kimberly who took position at the back of our little troupe.

As we walked away, I looked back over my shoulder just in time to see the portal close behind us. The technician would open it again in exactly forty-eight hours, and then again every four hours after that for three days in case we were delayed for some reason. Knowing that didn't stop the feeling of finality as the portal winked out of existence, though. I swallowed again.

That next several hours consisted of little more than walking and taking in the alien scenery. It was like going to the zoo for the first time. Everywhere I looked there was a new plant to be discovered. And, more rarely, a new animal. Creatures scampered through the grass ahead of us or, as we moved into a forest, up and down tree trunks on either side. Some of the creatures had fur, but most appeared scaled. Each was fascinatingly unique, and Johan often had to pull us away to keep us moving.

There was one surprise, though.

"How come there are no birds?" Vinnie asked.

I blinked. I hadn't even noticed their lack, though now that Vinnie mentioned it, Alcor Five was quite a bit quieter than I expected. I'd gotten used to hearing the occasional bird call or the like back on earth. Here, there was almost nothing.

"No birds here," Kimberly replied. "The Reptuses would eat them all."

We stopped briefly for food at local noon. As we ate, Johan pulled out his navigation tablet and checked it. "We're getting close," he said.

"How much farther?" Vinnie asked. He looked nervous. For that matter, I was beginning to get pretty keyed up myself.

Johan shrugged. "Best estimate is another five kilometers or so. The nests are never exactly where the scouting reports put them though, so be alert. You remember what to look for?"

We all nodded.

"Raised ground like a hill or a mountain peak," Carl said. "Fallen trees in a cluster near the top, and a smell like ammonia."

"All I know is this sucker better have good treasure," Vinnie said, grinning mischievously. "A couple thousand gold pieces and magic sword or two. Right guys?"

He laughed, but his mirth quickly faded as no one else joined in.

Kimberly looked at him askance and rolled her eyes.

Johan was less gentle. Standing, he pointed at Vinnie sternly and said in a tone that was nearly a growl, "This isn't a game. Get your head out of your ass and into reality, Vinnie. You're liable to get someone killed."

Vinnie shriveled under their disapproving looks. After a moment, he nodded, but I could tell he was a bit pissed off.

We set off again a few minutes later, expecting to reach the nest within an hour or so. But three hours later, we still hadn't seen any sign.

"Where is it?" I grumped after we passed yet another promising hill that ended up not being the spot.

Carl shrugged.

Johan pulled out his navigation tablet again. "Any moment now," he said.

Just then I heard a loud roar from somewhere ahead, and I froze. Beside me, Vinnie breathed, "Was that...?"

"Sure was," Johan said, his tone considerably more cheerful that it had been a moment before. Turning to face us, he grinned. I'd never seen him crack a smile before. "You gents ready?"

Before we could respond one way or another, the roar sounded again, considerably louder than the first time. Then a rhythmic beating sound intruded into the forest's sudden silence. A shadow passed overhead as something huge blocked out the sun for a moment. Then yet another roar forced me to clasp my hands over my ears. It was deafening!

The dragon flew away to the north. It was easy to tell

which direction it was going from watching the shadow's movement. I tried to move, but couldn't. That thing was BIG!

Then Vinnie sprinted away, running at top speed after the dragon and whooping at the top of his lungs.

"Sonofa... Get back here!" shouted Johan. Kimberly said something very un-ladylike at the same time. Then we all took off running after Vinnie.

Problem was, Vinnie had been an all-state sprinter in high school. He could outrun every wide receiver on the football team, but he hated football so he went out for track instead. He got an athletic scholarship to college. And though he wasn't in the same shape now as he had been then, hell none of us were, he still placed near the top of our age range in running events. He quickly left us behind, and before long all we had to follow him by was the sound of breaking twigs and branches, and his loud whooping. Finally, after several long minutes of chasing after him, we burst out of the woods into a broad meadow and pulled up short

There, crouched about fifty or sixty meters away in the middle of the meadow, was the dragon.

It was huge, far larger than I expected, maybe forty meters from head to tail. It sat atop its lunch, a creature the size of a horse that lay pinned beneath the talons of the dragon's front legs. Although maybe legs was the wrong word, since although the dragon supported itself on them, they were also a part of its wings. As we entered the meadow, the dragon bit off a piece of flesh the size of a teenager from the creature and began wolfing it down.

"My God..." I breathed in between panting breaths.

Then I noticed Vinnie, standing a few paces in front of us. He stood perfectly still for a moment. Then his chest expanded as he drew a deep breath and nocked an arrow.

Vinnie drew back on the bowstring.

"Stop!" Kimberly exclaimed, and she leapt toward him. But she was too late, as the pair of them tumbled onto the ground a heartbeat after he loosed the arrow.

I watched the arrow fly straight and true toward the dragon. As it flew, I praised Vinnie in my mind for his marksmanship. Then it struck the dragon in its side, just below where the wing flesh merged with its hip, and a flash of flame erupted as the explosive charge detonated.

The dragon roared and the meat in its mouth flew out as though spat. It staggered and turned toward us. For a moment, its eyes met mine, or at least I thought they did. Then it roared again and, with a push from its hind legs and a flap of its wings, hurled itself toward us.

"Get down!" Johan shouted. In my peripheral vision, I saw him raising his plasma rifle as I dove to the ground.

Then the dragon passed overhead and pulled straight up, flapping its wings to accelerate itself vertically. Its tail whipped around as the beast flew past and struck Johan before he got his rifle to his shoulder. He flew backward and landed back among the trees somewhere.

I rolled over onto my back. Looking straight up, I could see the dragon winging its way upward until it leveled off several hundred meters above us. For a moment, I thought it was going to flee. Then it banked around and dove.

"It's coming back!" I shouted and bounded to my feet.

"Into the woods," Kimberly ordered.

She didn't have to say it twice. We hustled beneath the cover of the trees, making it there a heartbeat before the dragon swooped down, its rear talons skimming the ground in an attempt to grab one of us. Then it flapped upwards again, roaring as it went.

"Holy cow," Carl said, his voice trembling. Personally, I

would have used a stronger word, but Carl had this thing about profanity.

"We should be safe here," Kimberly said. She peered upward, no doubt trying to follow the dragon's movement through the forest canopy. Then, after a minute or so, she turned venomous eyes onto Vinnie. "You jackass, what the hell were you thinking?"

Vinnie looked taken aback. "What are you talking about? We came to hunt the thing didn't we?"

Kimberly drew herself up. I could see her muscles tense, and for a moment I thought sure she was going to hit him. Then she breathed a curse and turned away, stalking over toward where Johan lay sprawled on the ground.

"What?" Vinnie said again, looking from me to Carl in confusion.

"Dude," I said, "combined tactics. Teamwork. Remember what we talked about for the last week?"

"I…"

Kimberly cut off whatever Vinnie was going to say with a terse request for assistance. I hurried over and so did Carl. Vinnie followed at a distance. When I got to Kimberly's side, I had to bite back a curse of my own. Johan was unconscious, and his breastplate was caved in on his right side. Blood seeped out slowly from beneath the armor, and a trickle flowed out of the side of his mouth.

"Oh no," I said as I squatted down beside Johan. "Will he be ok?"

Kimberly shook her head. "Not if we don't get him to medical treatment." She drew a deep breath and stood. "This expedition is over. We're heading back to the portal coordinates right now."

Of all people, Carl was the one who raised an objection.

"Like hell," he said. "We paid good money to come here and…"

"I wasn't asking," Kimberly growled. As she glared at Carl, the image of her taking us down with the ease of a child stomping out an anthill came to mind, a memory of our first evening of sparring training. That had been humbling, to say the least. "Now make yourselves useful," she went on, "and go find some long sticks that we can use to make a litter."

That took a bit of doing, but after a little while we found enough fallen limbs to make something. It required the use of our only tent to make something to lay Johan on between the limbs, but after a bit of work we had a litter. It probably would have been faster if the dragon hadn't flown overhead five or six more times and distracted us with its roaring each time.

Moving Johan onto the litter was in one sense easier and in another more difficult than I thought it would be. He weighed less here, but whatever advantage that gave me and Carl in lifting him was more than made up for by the fact that we had to worry about exacerbating his injuries if we did something wrong while getting him into position. But eventually we got him properly settled.

Johan's navigation tablet was crushed, but fortunately Kimberly had one as well. As soon as we had Johan on the litter, she gestured for us to follow her and set off toward the portal site. Watching her move out, I was torn between knowing that heading back was the right thing to do and desiring to stay and finish what we'd started. Although truth to tell, after seeing the dragon up close, a large part of me had no desire to ever come near that thing again. So after only a moment's hesitation, I hefted the handles of Johan's litter and followed Kimberly.

It was slow going. The litter was heavy, making it necessary for us to swap out dragging it. The rolling terrain, so picturesque not so long ago, became the source of many curses as we struggled to maneuver the litter up and down the various hills. By the time the sun began to set in the eastern sky, something that was exceedingly off-putting when I stopped to think about it, we had only gone a few kilometers.

I flopped to the ground. My legs and shoulders trembled from the day's exertions, my mouth was dry from thirst, and the growls from my stomach were almost as loud as... Another roar echoed through the woods. Much softer than before, more distant. But still it sent a shiver up my spine.

"Jesus that thing was big," Carl said as he sat down next to me.

Kimberly squatted down next to the litter to examine Johan. After a moment, she looked over at Carl and replied, "I've never seen a Reptus that large. They normally top out around twenty-five meters in length."

So we really had found a monster. For some reason, hearing that made me feel a bit better about leaving.

"How's he looking?" I asked.

She shrugged. "He's hanging in there, but his breathing is getting worse."

Over to the side, away from the rest of us, Vinnie sat down silently. He hadn't said a word since we left the scene of our encounter with the dragon. That wasn't like him.

"You ok, buddy?"

Vinnie looked at me, and I was shocked to see tears in his eyes. "I'm sorry guys," he said, his voice breaking. "I screwed this whole thing up."

"Yeah, you sure did." Kimberly stood from her squatting position and glared at him. Hard. Vinnie's lips compressed and for a second I thought he was going to fire back at her. Then his shoulders slumped and he hung his head.

"Jesus, Kimberly. He made a mistake. He didn't intend…"

Kimberly cut me off. "Didn't intend?? Who gives a damn what he intended? Look what happened because of him!" She pointed toward Johan and glared at me for a few seconds. Then she turned and stomped away, very quickly moving out of sight behind a cluster of trees.

A long silence followed that was punctuated by soft sobs coming from Vinnie. I glanced over at Carl and saw him chewing on his lip the way he did when he was contemplating something that troubled him. I felt the same way. I wanted to let Vinnie off the hook, but it was hard to deny Kimberly's words.

Abruptly, Carl stood up. "I'm going to go get some wood for a fire."

That left me and Vinnie alone. I had no idea what to say, so I voiced the first thing that came to mind. "It could be worse, brother."

Vinnie looked up at me. His eyes were red, his cheeks wet with tears. "How?"

I gestured toward the sky and managed as light a tone as I could. "It could be raining."

Vinnie's eyes widened incredulously and his jaw dropped. For once, it seemed, he had no comeback. We sat there for a moment, mutually speechless. Then we both burst out laughing, a long, throaty, therapeutic series of guffaws that left us both panting for breath and wiping our eyes.

Carl came back just then, carrying an armload of branches and twigs. He looked askance at us as he sat the firewood down over to the side of our little gathering spot. "What's so funny?"

I couldn't help it. I started laughing again. Vinnie joined in immediately. The mildly offended expression on Carl's face as he sniffed and went about getting the fire set up was priceless.

My chuckles subsided after a moment, and I got up to help Carl. Before long, we had a merry little fire going. And just in time, too, because the sunset was a lot quicker than I figured it would be. The growing gloom of twilight soon settled in and the temperature began to drop, but we were nice and comfy around our fire.

Until Kimberly came back.

"What the hell are you doing?" she thundered as she walked into view. "Put that fire out!"

"Wha-?" Carl began, but she bowled right over him.

"Christ, didn't any of you listen to anything last week?" she snarled as she kicked dirt onto the fire. "The Reptus has extremely keen vision. It'll..."

"...see even a small fire from a dozen kilometers away," I finished. "You said not to light a fire before the hunt because it could make it wary or induce it to move to another area. The hunt's done now, so who cares?"

She glared at me for a moment, her foot raised in mid-kick. Then she sighed, nodded, and lowered her foot slowly to the ground. "You're right. But what we didn't tell you, because most of the time it doesn't matter, is that an enraged Reptus will sometimes see a fire and decide to attack. No one knows why, though some have hypothesized that they've come to associate flames with hunting parties."

Across the fire pit from me, Vinnie began choking on the swig of water he had just swallowed. "What??"

Kimberly shrugged. "It's up to you if you want to keep it. I'll be sleeping over there." She made a vague gesture towards the woods, now pitch dark in the moonless night. The three of us traded glances, then, our decision made, we wasted no time in helping her smother the fire.

It was a long, chilly, uncomfortable night. We slept huddled together in a group surrounding Johan's litter. Or at least we tried to sleep. I probably got an hour of actual quality shut-eye; the rest of the night I spent struggling to ignore the cold or pretending to be comfortable while longing for the relative luxury of the tent that we'd used to make the litter.

Finally, dawn came.

No one hesitated to get up despite the fact that we had been unable to rest properly. The promise of a return to the luxuries of modern living was all the motivation we needed to get up and get moving as swiftly as possible.

Firm resolve and determination to cover ground quickly faded, though, before the onslaught of sore muscles, a heavy load, and difficult terrain. Morning turned to noon and we'd barely made eight kilometers. The portal was still another fifteen kilometers away, give or take. There was no way we'd make it there before nightfall.

"On the bright side," Vinnie huffed as he took his turn dragging the litter, "the tech wasn't planning to open the portal again until tomorrow anyway."

That was true enough, but it wasn't much comfort. It would have been nice to not have more walking to look forward to in the morning.

We made camp that night in a valley that was tucked between a trio of hills. A small stream ran through the valley and provided a supply of fresh water, once it was purified of course. But there was another reason Kimberly chose it, one that made me forget all the rotten things I'd thought about her in the past.

"We'll build a fire tonight," she announced shortly after we all collapsed onto the turf. She grinned as we looked at her, no doubt seeing the complete surprise I felt etched into all of our faces. Whatever she saw, it made her chuckle. She gestured toward the three hills and said, "The hills will shield the light from the Reptus' eyes unless he's almost directly over-head. And if he's there…"

"…we've got bigger problems than a campfire," Carl finished.

"Exactly. Besides," she said, glancing at Johan, "It'll do Johan good to have more warmth tonight."

And so, when I woke up the next morning I felt one hell of a lot better. It's amazing the assistance a bit of warmth will give toward getting a good night's sleep. And of course, a good night's sleep can make all the difference. I'd once heard a phrase: sleep is a weapon. That morning, I felt the truth of that statement, as I felt recharged, ready and eager to take on the world. Looking around at my friends, I could tell Vinnie and Carl felt, if not totally ready to go, at least less beat down than they had the previous day.

By Kimberly's calculations, we would likely reach the portal coordinates a bit before noon, local time. Well after the first planned portal opening, but only a half hour before the second. Perfection. When we emerged from the forest a couple kilometers from the hill where the portal would open, and especially when we began trudging toward it, my spirits soared. We'd made it. In a very few minutes, the portal would open and we'd all return to earth. The very first thing I planned to do was get a hot chocolate. The others wore large grins as they, too, no doubt contemplated their return to modern luxury and what to do when they got there.

So naturally things chose that particular moment to fall apart completely.

I had gotten ahead of Carl, who was pulling the litter, and turned around to say something to him. My words stuck in my throat, though, as I focused on the sky behind him. There, winging swiftly toward us no more than a kilometer away, was the dragon. I raised my hand to point at it and opened my mouth to scream a warning, but the distant, though still thunderous, roar from the beast reached us before I could say a word.

Everyone frozen in place.

"Oh, no," breathed Vinnie. He turned his head slightly to look at me, and only me. It was almost as though he couldn't physically bring himself to look at the approaching creature so he looked at me instead. It pained me to not be able to offer comfort this time.

"It's coming," I said in as close to a matter-of-fact tone as I could muster.

The dragon was about three-quarters of a kilometer away now. The tree line was about half a kilometer away. We'd never make it.

"Spread out," Kimberly ordered. I looked her way and saw that she had unslung her plasma rifle and was checking its charge status. She did not have a hopeful expression on her face. "Take what cover you can when it attacks. And watch your ammo. Only take shots you're sure of."

She probably mean that for Vinnie more than Carl and me. Nonetheless, I noticed Carl pulling a spear out of his back harness. I did the same and pressed the control to extend it to its full length. Then I moved a bit away from the others and waited.

It wasn't a long wait. The dragon swooped in, issuing a deeper, more throaty roar that it had in the past. One of Vinnie's arrows struck it in the left shoulder, and the roar became more of a shriek. Its shoulder dipped, and it turned into a bank toward Vinnie. Then a ball of plasma from Kimberly's rifle struck it in the bely.

For a moment, I thought maybe the one-two punch of arrow and plasma rifle would be enough to finish the beast off.

Wishful thinking. It just made the dragon mad.

The beast quickly righted itself and dove toward the center of our little group. I hit the dirt and saw Carl hurl his spear upwards before my senses were obscured by wind-blown grass, the sound of beating wings, and the whooshing sound of the dragon's tale flailing through the air where I was just standing.

A solid THUD announced the dragon's momentary landing. Then a high-pitched shriek of pain and terror rang out. Kimberly! I boosted myself up onto my hands and knees in time to see the dragon toss its head and see Kimberly, whom it had apparently taken into its maw, fly through the air like a thrown-away trinket before landing in a heap. Then the dragon kicked itself airborne again. As it flew upwards, I was gratified to see three small trails of smoke streaming from its body, though that positive feeling faded quickly as it became clear that the wounds weren't slowing the dragon down much.

We had a moment's respite at least, so I rushed over to where Kimberly lay. She was a mess: several of the dragon's teeth had penetrated her armor, and she had a number of bleeding puncture wounds. Her left leg was twisted beneath her at an awkward angle, and she was not moving. But she still breathed and had a pulse. It was weak and thready, but it was there.

There wasn't time to tend to her, though.

"Here it comes again," shouted Vinnie.

Every fiber of my being shouted out for me to run. Staying here, out in the open like this, was foolishness. The dragon would just swoop in and take us out, and there was nothing we could do about it. To stay and fight was certain death. To flee though... I could make it. The odds were not great, but it was possible. If I waited until the last moment, when Vinnie and Carl engaged it...

Shame filled me, burying the urge to run beneath its weight and smothering it. I would not abandon my friends to their fate. If this was it, this was it, but I'd at least face it like a man. Glancing at my two best friends in the world, I saw fear in their faces, but on top of that a steely resolve. This is why we'd come here. After this, nothing would intimidate us again.

Shame gave way to adrenalin-laced euphoria as the dragon banked around and began its dive toward us. Not realizing what I was doing, I thrust my spear up into the air and issued a roar of my own. Guttural, emanating from something primal within me, it felt as though that roar itself would knock the creature from the sky. To either side, I heard Carl and Vinnie taking up the roar as well. Together we made a harmony of defiance, taunting the dragon in all its brutal beauty. Bring it on, foul beast. Bring it on.

The dragon headed straight toward us. Toward me. Our eyes met, just as they had in the meadow a day and a half earlier. Its maw opened as it streaked closer. It was death on the wing, come for me. A part of my mind still screamed at me to duck, to run, but its screams went unanswered as the primal force within me refused to let loose its hold. The dragon's tongue ran over its teeth and its mouth opened even wider to scoop me up, a tasty morsel ripe for the eating.

Screaming a curse at approaching death, I drew back and threw my spear with every bit of power I could muster.

* * * * *

I'm told the salespeople at Dragon Safaris still talk about that throw. How my spear entered the dragon's mouth and exploded in its throat. How its dive turned into a crash. How it impacted the ground and slid toward me, coming to a halt less than a meter from where I stood. How neither I nor my friends moved a centimeter the whole time. I'm told they call it heroic, epic. A feat never to be repeated. How one man brought down the mightiest Reptus Volans ever recorded with a single throw of his spear.

I wouldn't know. I've never gone back there to find out. Carl, Vinnie, and I still get together for the ballgame, or for a while to try to meet girls, or these days to watch our sons play football, or for the other things that guys do together. We often talk about old times over a beer or two, but we never talk about that trip to Alcor Five. What is there to say? We went there. We experienced it. We survived it, even though in the end our guides did not. It is part of what made us into the men we came to be. But it is also the past, and we've learned to focus on the present and look to the future.

But sometimes, before I turn in for the night, I look up at the wall of my study at the horns of the mighty dragon where they are mounted for posterity, and I recall the primal song we sang together in that field on a far away world.

And I smile.

Grandfather's Pendant

One

W here the hell is it?" Jiles said.

Jiles was clearly upset. He pawed through his belongings frantically, throwing various and sundry personal articles all over his corner of the tent in his search for…whatever it was. He was normally the neatest of Larian's tent mates, hardly ever leaving anything out of place at all, so something was clearly wrong.

"Jiles…"

The slender man shot a glare at Larian that made his teeth shut with a soft click, stifling what he was about to say.

Clearing his throat, Larian tried a different tactic. He began gathering up the items that Jiles had strewn around and brought them back to Jiles' corner, where he folded then stacked them neatly.

Jiles watched Larian doing this for a few minutes, in between soft curses and more pawing through what few belongings he had left that were not scattered all over the place, his expression growing more and more annoyed. Finally, he straightened and scowled.

"What are you doing?"

Larian shrugged. "If the Sergeant were to step in here right now, we would all get latrine duty for the next week." He left the rest unsaid, instead focusing on carefully folding one of Jiles' undershirts.

Jiles blinked then looked around the tent. His eyes went wide and he flushed with embarrassment. "Oh," he said weakly, his tone noticeably mollified from its earlier angry snap. "Good thinking." He bent over to pick up a pair of breaches and added, "Thanks."

Jiles folded the breaches and handed them to Larian, who slipped them back into Jiles' bag that he used for clean laundry. "What are you looking for?" Larian asked, mystified at the other man's behavior. He had only known Jiles for a few weeks, but he was normally even-keeled and cheerful, not given to hysterics.

A brief period of silence followed. Jiles' lips compressed as though he was fighting back some great emotion, then he turned away and began picked up a bunch of discarded socks. Larian watched him patiently. Whatever Jiles was looking for, it must be important.

Finally, Jiles turned back around, cradling several pairs of socks in the nook of his elbow. The lean man walked over and dumped them into his dirty laundry bag without a word, then stood there, looking down into the bag for a moment. When he finally spoke, his voice was low, pensive.

"Yesterday at mail call a package arrived from my parents."

Larian nodded. "I remember seeing it. Something special,

wasn't it?" Not that any arriving mail was not special; mail call was always something to be treasured. But Jiles had seemed more moved than normal when he opened the package, though when the other men in the tent asked about it he gave only vague answers.

Jiles nodded. "My grandfather passed on," he said.

Larian felt a pang of sympathy and placed his hand on Jiles' shoulder, giving it a gentle squeeze. "I'm sorry, Jiles."

Jiles gave a little start and looked back at Larian, surprise written on his face. "Wha-?" Then understanding hit him and he nodded, smiling faintly. "I keep forgetting you haven't been here very long. No," Jiles shook his head sadly, "Grandfather has been ill for a while. I've known his time was near for almost a year now. I got some leave six months ago and we said our goodbyes, so it wasn't like it was a surprise."

Larian nodded in understanding. "But still..." He left the rest unsaid.

Another short period of silence followed as Jiles obviously took a moment to collect his thoughts. "He left me something - an old pendant that's been in the family for a long time. Mother packed it with the letter, and now I can't find it."

"Oh." That made more sense. "Well, when did you see it last?"

Jiles frowned for a moment, then sighed and slumped onto his cot. "I don't know. Sometime yesterday afternoon, before we went out to Mirasol."

Larian flinched slightly at the mention of the town's name. His liberty there had been...interesting. "You didn't bring it into town, did you?"

"I don't know. Maybe."

"Well," Larian said, trying to affect a cheerily confident tone, "we'll just have to retrace your steps. See if we can find it."

Jiles blinked and looked at Larian in surprise for a moment, then smiled gratefully.

The two men did not waste any more time with talk. They took a moment to don away their uniform doublets, simple but elegant garments of blue wool, trimmed in white, that carried their rank insignia on their upper arms and the insignia of their unit on their collars, and matching grey pants. Then they stomped on their boots and stepped out of the tent into the camp beyond.

The Company's camp was smaller than the Regimental encampment Larian had become used to. Oh, it was still orderly and tidy, laid out in quadrants just as the Regimental camp had been, with each platoon housed together in its own area - cavalry separate from pikeman, who were separate from the archers and the scouts. But the feel of the place was different. Morale was higher. Not that it had ever been low; it was hard to be bitter under the Commander they had. Still, for whatever reason everyone walked a bit taller, with a bit more of a swagger about them. It was hard not to, considering their recent victory.

They passed the Company Commander's tent in the center of the camp and veered left toward the camp entrance, pausing only to salute one of the Platoon Leaders before he ducked into the Command tent. It was a short walk from there to the camp entrance. The guards nodded familiarly to them and waved them on without comment, though Larian thought he saw an amused twinkle in more than one eye.

"I think tales of our exploits have made it back here," Jiles remarked as they left the guards behind.

Larian smirked and chuckled. He should have known Jiles would notice the guards' amusement as well. "Guess so," he replied, and cringed when he realized he sounded a bit embarrassed.

Jiles just laughed, but blessedly did not twist the knife.

The Liberty wagon stood a short distance away from the camp entrance. Larger than most, it boasted a team of six draft horses and a cargo area that could carry a score or more, depending on how close people felt like sitting to each other. Even though it was not due to depart for a half hour, there was already a fair-sized group of men waiting.

And no wonder. It was not often that soldiers in a deployed unit were allowed liberty away from camp. Jiles had never seen it happen before, or so he told Larian two days ago when the word came down about it, but the older members of Larian's unit had experienced it, though infrequently.

But these were not ordinary circumstances. The Regiment had just won a great victory, one that from sheer numbers alone they should have lost easily. But the Commander was a clever one, and he managed to outfox the Mar Tabban leaders easily - or he made it look easy from Larian's perspective at least - and the enemy incursion was stopped handily. That was not to say the fighting itself was easy; Larian had been in a number of hairy situations over the three days of battle. But it turned out well.

And so the Commander decreed a Liberty week as a reward to the men and as a celebration, something even the oldest veterans had never seen before. A day, maybe two…but a week?

The rules were simple. One company at a time would depart the main camp and make its way to Mirasol, a moderate-sized town two days' march west. Upon arrival, the company would have a week to allow its men liberty.

The Company Commander decreed the camp would be manned at all times. Everyone would muster in the morning and take care of basic camp upkeep. Then all but the duty guardsmen and other essential personnel were given the day for themselves. Even better, each day a few would be allowed to spend the night in Mirasol, and would not have to muster until the day after their night pass. The overnight pass would rotate through the men so that most everyone got a night away. It was like gold.

Fortune decided that Larian and Jiles should have the overnight pass together, but not until two days from now. That had not stopped them for heading out to Mirasol for an evening of entertainment. The last night's revelry had lasted until the very last Liberty wagon departed Mirasol for the camp, an hour after midnight. As he and Jiles settled into the group awaiting the wagon's departure, Larian mulled over that fact and grimaced. There would be a lot of ground to cover if they were to find Jiles' heirloom.

When he first saw Mirasol yesterday, Larian had mixed feelings. It was a far sight larger than the town, little more than a village really, where he had grown up. But compared with the stronghold at Tel Cerelon, where the Martial Academy was housed, Mirasol was modest at best. But the town had quickly grown on him. The people were friendly and cheerful, although a small cynical voice in his head whispered that probably had as much to do with the coin the soldiers spent while on Liberty as from any genuine pleasure at seeing them. Real or feigned, though, the townsfolk's welcome lifted Larians spirits considerably.

Time seemed to drag as he and Jiles awaited the wagon team's return, and then during the hour-long ride to Mirasol. Larian was eager to get back to the town, but Jiles was practically jumping out of his skin with anxiety. No wonder, considering the circumstances, but Larian had never seen him this keyed up before, not even when the platoon had been cut off during the battle and they all wondered if they were going to make it out alive. Larian queried Jiles about it once, and received a vague shrug along with an evasive reply, so he decided to let it lie.

The Liberty Wagon dropped them off in Mirasol's central square, a half-acre of manicured park surrounded on all sides by the official town buildings, shops, and a few inns. Roads branched off from the square at the four points of the compass, leading to the town's various districts.

From what Larian had seen the previous evening, there was not a whole lot of interest past the square, though. The shops quickly faded in favor of residential areas to the west and north, tanneries and merchant warehouses to the east, and temples and the guards' barracks to the south. For a young soldier looking for a good time, the action was all in the Inns. And the brothels, which were also located in the south side of town, or so Larian had heard. Thoughts of Rosaline back at home kept Larian's interest away from those establishments, but others had returned to camp with tales of those ladies' skills.

Larian felt his face flush at the memory and he cleared his throat, pointedly not looking to the south side of the square. "Right," he said. "Where to now?"

Jiles looked around for a minute then nodded toward the east side of the square. "The Horned Hare," he said. "That's where we went first."

That seemed logical enough. Larian followed without comment.

They passed through the carefully manicured park, complete with its fountains and statues, presumably of famous people form Mirasol's history, though Larian did not see any names he recognized. It was a walk of only a few minutes, but in that time the eastern side of the square changed from its normal peaceful afternoon demeanor into one of bustling anger. A crowd began to gather - out front of their target

Inn, Larian noticed. He frowned, anxiety beginning to rise within him.

"What's going on?" Jiles asked as they stepped from the park onto the cobblestones of the square in front of the Inn, echoing Larian's thoughts.

A slight man, local by his dress, glanced over at the Larian and Jiles and spat onto the street. "A couple of your fellows, that's what. You soldier boys don't know how to keep it in your pants, do you?"

Larian blinked, trading a cautious glance with Jiles. It was awfully early for that sort of thing, wasn't it?

"We should probably see if we can help," Jiles said, his tone becoming grim, the way it did before a fight.

He and Larian pushed their way through the growing crowd, earning themselves several angry looks. Most of the looks mellowed when the people giving them saw their uniforms, Larian was gratified to see. Except for one man, a short but solid-looking fellow with a bushy black beard and grey eyes. When Larian brushed past him, he turned with a scowl. Then he saw Larian and Jiles - really Jiles - and his scowl turned into a snarl.

"You!" the man growled and he reached out and grabbed Jiles by the lapels of his tunic. Jiles' eyes widened in surprised shock as he found himself dragged off his feet by the shorter man. He opened his mouth to make a reply, but before he could speak, the man released his grip on Jiles' tunic, drew back and drove his fist into Jiles' belly.

Jiles dropped, his breath exploding from his lungs in a gurgling groan.

Larian froze for a second in shock at the sudden attack, then sprang forward toward the attacker. His progress was halted quickly when something struck him on the side of the head. Larian fell to the ground as well, seeing stars for a few moments. When he regained his equilibrium, he looked up to see the original attacker crouched down in front of Jiles, who still gasped and coughed, trying to get his breath back; he was in no condition to fight.

"Don't ever show your face around here again," growled the bearded man, then he pulled Jiles' head up by his hair and slugged Jiles in the face. He dropped again.

The man and his companions, there were three of them from what Larian could figure out, disappeared quickly into the crowd. Almost as quickly as they left, the crowd began to disperse. Within minutes, Larian and Jiles were left alone in the street except for a few lingering passers-by.

"What the hell was that?" Larian managed to prop himself up on his elbows as he spoke, but could not go much farther than that because the world began to spin around him.

Jiles shook his head slowly, pressing his hand to his cheek, where the bearded man's fist had struck him. He did not try to sit up. "No idea. Who was that guy?"

Larian shrugged in response. No answer was forthcoming from any of the few remaining people standing nearby either, so they would have to be content with their attackers' identity remaining a mystery.

Over the next couple minutes, Larian and Jiles got to their feet. The passers-by did not offer any assistance, verbal or otherwise. In fact, they steered well clear of the two young men, despite it being the middle of the afternoon. That was odd; for that matter, where were the Town Guards? People just did not get assaulted in the middle of the day without it being noticed and acted upon…did they?

The Horned Hare was only a few steps away, so they ventured inside to take stock. The taproom was not very busy, but that was not unusual considering the hour. They settled down on a bench at a table near the window and silently began to tend their bruises. They were quickly interrupted by the arrival of a young, apron-wearing barmaid with a cheery smile that turned a plain face into one of simple beauty and sparkling green eyes. Her smile faded a bit as she saw their condition.

"What happened to you two?" she asked, her voice concerned.

Jiles grunted something that sounded grumpy. Larian could not blame him, but there was no cause to take it out on the barmaid. He managed as much a smile as he could and replied, "I'm not entirely sure." Larian then told her what had happened and her eyes went wide, with shock, Larian supposed at first.

"You boys better leave town. Now," she said, glancing toward the taproom door and licking her lips. She was not shocked, she was frightened!

Jiles looked up at her and scowled. "Because of some jerk who can't see past a uniform?"

The barmaid looked at him as she would at a stupid schoolboy. "He was not just some jerk. That man you described sounds like one of Yohan Semilon's men. He's…" She looked around quickly, though there was no one else around to hear it. "He's a very rough man."

Jiles snorted. The barmaid's expression became, if anything, even more severe and frightened than before.

"What was the deal with that crowd?" Larian asked.

The girl shrugged. "No idea. Someone outside began shouting about soldiers cheating him. Then another guy piped up that some soldiers had dishonored his daughter. Next thing we knew, that crowd had gathered."

"They left very quickly," Larian said.

She nodded. "Yeah, it was strange. They all of a sudden stopped shouting and everyone left. It was almost like…"

She stopped, looking at them with wide eyes again.

"Like someone staged that crowd just to provide cover," Jiles finished. He sounded resigned, but his lips were compressed into an expression of towering fury. Larian had only seen that look on his face a few times, but he knew it meant trouble for whomever caused it.

Jiles' implication was not lost on Larian, though it seemed a bit thin. "No," he said, shaking his head. "There's no way that was just for you...for us. That doesn't make any sense."

"I would agree except the timing is a bit too much of a coincidence." Jiles looked at the barmaid, and asked, "Who is this Semilon? What is his business?"

The girl bit her lip and glanced around again, clearly not happy with the way the conversation had turned. She delayed answering for a few seconds, making Larian think she was going to just leave. When she finally spoke, it was in a hushed whisper.

"They say if a crime happens in town, he's behind it. Or at least he approved it. But the Guards have never been able to prove anything. He runs a gambling house on the east side. I hear it can get rather rough sometimes."

Jiles' face went pale as the girl finished. He looked away from her, toward the window, and muttered, "Bugger me."

The girl flushed and looked away. Surely the language had not offended her, working in a taproom as she did? Larian cleared his throat and held out a silver penny. "Thank you. Can you bring us a couple mugs of ale? Keep the change."

The girl's eyes widened: it was a very nice tip. She bobbed her head, made a half-curtsy, and hurried off to the bar.

As soon as she was out of earshot, Larian leaned forward over the table. "What's wrong?"

"I remember what happened," Jiles replied, sounding a bit sick.

That could not be good. Larian waited, not wanting to intrude until Jiles was ready.

In the intervening moments, the girl returned with two foaming tankards, which she set down on the table with another cheery smile, this one a bit forced unless Larian missed his guess. Jiles raised his tankard and took a long drink. When he finally came up for air, it did not look as though he felt any better. His eyes were haunted, defeated.

"I went gambling last night," Jiles said.

"Yes, I know. So what...oh. Oh no."

Jiles nodded. "I was up, but the stakes got larger as the night moved on and I was nearing my limit. There was this one guy with an obvious tell, and I thought sure I could take him. So," he took another drink, looking thoroughly miserable, then continued, "I put everything I had down on one last hand. But he had more money than I did, and he raised me. I could not fold and lose it all, so..."

"You wagered your grandfather's heirloom."

Jiles shook his head. "No. I managed to convince him I had more money in my room at the Inn. The owner staked me, and we finished out the hand." He hung his head. "I lost."

"That explains why Semilon's angry. When he found out you had no more money..."

Jiles shook his head. "I didn't give him the chance. I ran. Beat down the guard at the door and ran."

That triggered a memory for Larian: Jiles sprinting to catch up with the Liberty Wagon as it pulled out of the square on its last run back to camp. He had presumed the other man was just running late, nothing more.

"We'd better get back to camp. They won't be satisfied with a light beating."

Jiles shook his head, more emphatically. "No. Not until I

find my grandfather's pendant."

"It's probably just in another bag at camp. We'll…"

Jiles leaned forward, nearly snarling. "No! I had it with me, in my pouch. I remember that now. But when I got back to the wagon my pouch was gone. I didn't think anything of it at the time, since I was out of money, but…"

That sinking feeling returned in Larian's gut. "You think it's in the gambling den."

Jiles nodded.

Larian looked away and thought the situation over for a moment. This could only end badly, that was clear. The smart play was to get back to camp and forget about it. Heirlooms were lost all the time. He almost said as much, but looking at Jiles' stricken face, Larian found he was unable to force the words from his lips. Wonderful. He was going to regret this; they both were.

"Alright. Let's go get it back."

Jiles blinked, looking surprised for a second. Then a grateful smile spread across his face.

Two

The Bluffing Lass sat caddy-corner from a warehouse and a tannery. A sign hanging over the door featured a buxom beauty with rosy cheeks and a sly smile on her face, holding a hand of cards over her bodice. It was actually fairly inviting, and certainly played up the irony of the establishment's name. The building itself was squat, but well constructed and maintained. It was painted in lively colors that managed to make it look cheerful, at least superficially.

The odors from the tannery definitely lowered the attractiveness of the area, but overall it did not look as though this place was a hive of scum and villainy. But appearances can be deceiving.

It was with a certain amount of trepidation that Larian stepped up to the gambling house's entrance.

Jiles would be instantly set upon the moment he set foot inside, but Larian did not expect to be recognized, so the reconnaissance fell to him. All the same, as he reached out for the door handle, it almost felt as though he was walking into an ambush. Larian glanced up at the sky, still deep blue despite the beginnings of sunset, and said a silent prayer that this would go well. Or at least not be a total disaster. Then he stepped inside.

And stopped dead in shock.

Inside was like another world, one of opulence and indulgence. The room was lit by numerous brightly-burning chandeliers that hung from the ceiling every few paces. Rich tapestries depicting the hunt, or famous battles, or happy people taking their leisure, lined the walls. Thick carpets of deep red covered the floor, muffling his footsteps. The scent of fine incense filled the air, along with the sounds of laughter and boisterous conversation intermixed with shouts of victory and groans of loss. Tables for the various games, each surrounded by a crowd of people in clothes ranging from the finest silks to the poorest wool, were scattered throughout the room. Serving girls, dressed in tightly-fitting red gowns with golden lace in suggestive places, roamed between the tables, carrying trays filled with drinks of all varieties. Against the wall to the right was a thick wooden bar with polished brass taps for the various casks that were stacked behind it. A pair of large swinging doors dominated the far wall, beneath a sign that read "High Stakes". A smaller door, made of metal with a sliding viewport at eye level, stood next to the bar.

Larian had a notion of what a gambling house would be like, before he entered. This was not it. The place looked almost respectable.

"You gonna gawk or you gonna play, lad?"

The gruff voice drew Larian's gaze away from the room to the man standing to his right. Tall, bald, and bulging with muscles, he had a scar that ran the length of his right cheek and a tattoo of a star on the left side of his neck. He wore a simple red tunic that was trimmed in golden thread and black pants tucked into heavy workboots. His face seemed made for scowling, though he had a twinkle in his eye as he looked Larian up and down - amusement?

Larian cleared his throat. "Play, I suppose."

"Thought so. Table minimum's two pennies here. Max bet is five marks."

"Five marks?"

The bouncer's eyes narrowed. "You wanna bet more, gotta go in back. Back's got an entrance fee, though."

"Oh. Right." Larian had no intention of betting even that much, but it was probably best not to reveal that. "Thanks."

He set off toward the bar. Best to take a look around and get a feel for things before committing to a particular game. He supposed.

"Nice shirt," quipped the bouncer as he moved away. "Hate to see you lose it."

Larian glanced back and forced a grin that he hoped was confident onto his lips. The bouncer met his gaze and smirked. So much for the confidence.

The bartender was a man of average height and build, with thick black hair that he wore cut short. He wore the same colors as the other employees: red with gold thread. As Larian slid onto a stool, the bartender gave him a once-over and grunted.

"What'll it be?"

Larian glanced at the casks and bottles behind the bar but saw only names that he knew to be expensive or that he did not recognize at all. He hesitated for a moment, then shrugged. "Ale."

The bartender nodded with a snort and turned to his taps,

at the far end of the bar from Larian.

While he waited for his drink, Larian turned on his stool to survey the room again. From what he could tell, there were three of four different games: two card games of some variety or other, though in truth it could have been the same game for all Larian knew, a game of dice, and a game that seemed to revolve around a great spinning wheel with a ball that bounced around on it.

Just then he hit upon the great flaw in his reconnaissance plan. He had no idea how to play any of them.

Three

W ell, I'm broke."

Jiles looked askance at Larian as he sat down. Their tent seemed a bit more cramped than usual, even with just the two of them present. Jiles had come back on the liberty wagon as soon as Larian left for The Bluffing Lass. No sense in pushing his luck, after all. Not until it was necessary, anyway.

"That was fast."

Larian shrugged. "That dice game was more tricky than it looked."

Jiles whistled softly through his teeth. "I guess I should have warned you." He flopped back onto his rack and blew out a deep breath. "Well so much for that, then. Bugger me."

"Not so fast. I'm broke, not clueless."

"Huh?"

Larian rolled his eyes. "I kept my eyes open while I was in there. One of the bouncers wore a pretty distinctive necklace. An eagle on the wing with sapphire eyes. That the one?"

Jiles sat bolt upright on his rack, his eyes widening in recognition. "By Deus," he began. Then he stopped, swallowed, and began again. "That's it. Which bouncer was it?"

"Short guy. Skinny. Blond hair and a short goatee. Not the sort of guy I'd pick as a bouncer, if you ask me, but the others seemed to defer to him. I think his name was…"

"Roland."

Larian nodded. "Yep."

Jiles breathed a curse. "The other night, before things got all hazy, I remember seeing that guy take down two men at once who were giving the other bouncers trouble. He's fast. Real fast."

"So are you."

Jiles shrugged slightly but did not reply, instead looking aside toward the little box where he kept his mail.

"And besides, there's two of us, and we're not just a couple of drunk gamblers. I think we can probably handle him."

"What are you talking about?" Jiles looked back at Larian with an incredulous expression. "You don't mean to jump him on the street or something? We're not thugs."

"That wouldn't be my first choice, no. Maybe he would sell it…"

"No."

Larian blinked. "That would be the cleanest way."

"No. I'm not paying money for what's rightfully mine."

"Ok, but if you won't pay him and you don't want to just jump him, that doesn't leave a lot of options."

Jiles ground his teeth and leaned back on his elbows. After a moment of pondering, a small sly smile appeared on his face.

Larian's heart fell. He knew that smile, and even from the short time he had know him, Larian knew when Jiles smiled like that, he had something clever, but also very dangerous, in mind.

"Have you ever picked a lock?" Jiles asked.

Larian's jaw fell open in surprised shock.

Four

Larian pulled the cowl of his cloak down a bit lower. From where he stood, leaning against the trunk of a maple tree that grew in front of a small warehouse a block away from The Bluffing Lass, it would be difficult for anyone to spot him; the closest street lamp was a hundred feet away and it was not exactly a beacon. All the same, he could not help but feel exposed.

A trickle of sweat ran down his back and his heart raced, even though he had so far done little the entire evening expect stand there and watch. He was not cut out for the criminal life, apparently.

Jiles' plan was so ludicrous Larian still could not believe he had agreed to it.

It seemed simple enough. The next day, on their overnight liberty, they would go to town, get a room at an out-of-the-way inn, and lay low for the day. Then, come nightfall, they would stake out The Bluffing Lass until Roland left work. Then follow him home, wait for him to go to sleep, break into his place, and take back Jiles' pendant.

What could go wrong?

Larian saw dozens of things, and standing there against the tree, fully a dozen more sprang to mind as he waited.

This was a horrible idea.

But he had not been able to come up with anything better. It was not like they could go to the city watch. Hey, Mister Guardsman, my friend ran out on his bill at a local business and left a family heirloom there by mistake. Could you go get it back for him please? That would work out real well. With bargaining and assault ruled out - Larian really thought just buying back the cursed thing was the best route to take, but Jiles would not budge - there was nothing to it but to try Jiles' plan, stupid as it was. Larian just hoped it would not land them both in the stocks, or worse.

The night drew on. Dozens of people entered and left the gambling house, but Roland was not among them. Larian's anxiety faded gradually, replaced by boredom and growing fatigue. It was getting harder and harder to remain still without drifting off.

He felt something hard and rough impact the side of his head and jerked awake with a muttered oath, his hand darting instinctive to the hilt of the dagger he wore on his belt. A sword would not do: it would have drawn too many eyes in the Liberty wagon, and from the town guards. A dagger, though, that was easier to hide.

What just hit him? He looked around and blanched as he realized what happened. He had dozed off and his head hit the tree trunk. Larian muttered another oath at his lack of discipline and ran in place for a few seconds to get his blood flowing again. He needed to stay watchful.

Larian glanced up at the moons, visible together in the sky for the next week of their cycles, and tried to guess at the time. It must have been only a couple hours before dawn. The Bluffing Lass closed at two bells after midnight. Roland had to leave soon, unless he slept at work. That was a possibility neither he nor Jiles had thought of. It could mess everything up.

A high-pitched whistle, one of the songbird calls the scouts mimicked to pass information to each other, reached Larian's ears, and he perked up. Jiles had spotted their target.

There he was.

In his irritation at himself, Larian had missed Roland leaving the gambling house. He was now half a block away from the establishment, walking in Larian's direction. Jiles should be maneuvering to follow at a discrete distance; Larian just needed to stay out of sight until Roland passed, then he would rendezvous with Jiles and continue the pursuit.

That was great in theory, but in practice, his little bout with sleep left him away from the tree and exposed. If Roland had not seen him yet, he would very shortly. Larian was new at this, but he could imagine it would be suspicious if he just tried to hide right in front of the man.

Instead, he took a deep breath, drew the cowl down a little bit lower, and stepped out from beneath the tree.

Roland slowed as Larian drew nearer, following him with his eyes in a manner that shouted he knew what could happen on dark streets late at night. Larian put a bit of a stumble in his steps, trying to look as though he had consumed a few too many, and kept a good distance between Roland and himself, all the while praying to Deus he would not decide to start up a conversation.

He need not have worried. After the initial assessment, Roland seemed to dismiss him. As they passed each other,

Roland shot him one last glance, his shoulders tensing visibly as though he expected Larian to jump him from behind. But he never changed the length of his stride, and soon enough they were again two fellows walking their different ways.

Larian let out his breath and looked around for Jiles. He wouldn't be trailing Roland by more than a block, most likely less.

"What was that?"

Jiles' voice came from the shadows behind Larian and to his right. Larian spun to face him and saw only a darker patch among the shadows on the side of the building that looked vaguely human-like. With a quick shrug, he moved over to join his friend.

"I was away from the tree. Thought it was better than scurrying around all of a sudden."

Jiles pursed his lips slightly, then nodded. He knew improvisation was sometimes necessary, just as Larian did.

"One good thing though. He's still wearing the pendant. I saw it reflect the moonlight as we passed each other."

"Outstanding." Jiles sounded eager to be about their business.

Ahead of them, Roland turned to the left down a narrow side street. The sign at the intersection labelled it as "Porter Lane". As Larian and Jiles turned the corner, Larian immediately understood why.

The street ran between two large, warehouse-like buildings. The building on the right had a number of smokestacks, it looked like. Even though most of the interior lights were out, a few windows still shown with lamplight. Through them were visible large metal drums and running piping. Faintly at first, then stronger as they passed the midpoint of the building, the smell of hops wafted through the air.

"I love breweries," Jiles murmured.

Larian grinned, suppressing a chuckle.

His mirth faded quickly when he looked from the windows to the street ahead. Son of a...

"Where is he?"

Jiles swore, quite colorfully, Larian's words jerking him back to the task at hand.

They stopped and looked around, but as far as Larian could tell there was no sign of their quarry. How had they lost him so quickly? There was no way he could have gotten to the next intersection before they got here. Unless he had ducked into an alcove somewhere...

A barely perceptible rustling from behind was the first warning. The soft hiss of metal on leather followed almost immediately, then through his cowl Larian felt steel - sharp steel - against the back of his neck

"It's a little late for a stroll, boys." The voice was a smooth baritone, the accent educated, cultured.

Larian began to turn his head to get a look at the speaker - presumably Roland, but he preferred to know for certain - but the steel dug a bit deeper, penetrating the wool and pressing into his skin painfully. A wet trickle began to run down the back of his neck, and he knew the blade had begun to draw blood.

"Don't move an inch," the man said again. He paused, then added, "Either of you."

From the corner of his eye, Larian saw that Jiles was standing dead still as well. If it was just one man, he must have two blades. He was either very good for very foolish to do that. Larian suspected the former.

"Sir, we..." Jiles began.

"Shut up!" The interruption was accented by another increase in pressure on the blade. Larian gritted his teeth as the pain increased. His shirt was going to be ruined completely if this kept up.

"You picked the wrong man to rob," the man continued.

"We're not here to rob you." The lie flowed smoothly from Larian's lips. He did not even feel ironic in saying it.

"Oh really?"

"Yeah. We're just heading home is all," Jiles said.

A loud snort preceded another poke with the blade, mercifully, or not, in a different position on Larian's neck. "There are no homes down this way. Nothing this way til the end of town but warehouses. So why don't you try again."

Crap. That's what they get for skulking around in a town they did not know well. Now what?

"You've got something of mine." Jiles surprised Larian by coming straight to it. "I was hoping to buy it back." Oh so now he saw the wisdom in that? Larian almost shook his head in annoyance, but then he remembered the blade.

There was a long moment of silence, then the blade came off Larian's neck. He breathed a quick sigh of relief. Then the man stepped around in front of them, moving more quickly than Larian would have thought possible, at least not without losing control of himself.

But he didn't.

Roland slid smoothly around them on light feet that danced over the paving stones like he was on a stage. His blond hair seemed to shimmer in the moonlight. His narrowed eyes gazed at them intently as though daring them to make a move. He wore his work clothes, the red tunic with gold thread and black pants, beneath a flowing black cloak which he had thrown back over his shoulders to free up his arms. And he held a pair of long daggers, almost short swords in their own right, which he kept pointing at their faces.

"Lower the hoods," he commanded.

Larian complied, and he could see Jiles doing the same. Recognition flashed across Roland's face when he saw Larian. When Jile's face came out of the shadows, recognition quickly turned to disgust. And tightly wound anger.

"You! I ought to string you up and run you back to Yohan right now." He spat onto the ground at Jiles' feet. "You cost him a lot of money, boy."

Jiles scowled, then lowered his eyes for a moment. "Yeah. I'm not proud of that." He drew a deep breath and returned his gaze to Roland's. "My grandfather gave me that pendant when he died." He gestured at the eagle, dangling from a leather thong around Roland's neck. "It's been in the family for ten generations."

Roland blinked and his eyes flickered downward toward where the pendant dangled on his chest. He shifted slightly and the silver of the eagles glinted softly in the moonlight. "I found this on the street outside the club."

"I must have dropped it while I…"

"While you were running out on your bill." Roland sneered. "Why should I believe you?" He sniffed again. "Hell, I ought to bleed you right here, come to think of it." His muscles tensed as though he was about to move to do just that.

"How much?" Larian blanched as soon as he said that, because Roland's gaze returned to meet his. The man's eyes were cold, unfeeling, murderous. Despite the fact that his mouth had suddenly gone dry, Larian found himself swallowing.

"Fifty marks."

Fifty!? Larian shook his head. "No, how much for the pendant?"

"That's not for sale. But for fifty, maybe I won't tell Yohan I saw you tonight." His sneer turned positively vicious.

Larian looked over at Jiles, saw the muscles in his jaw tense momentarily, then relax. His entire body seemed to relax and his eyes went flat. Oh crap. Larian knew that look; Jiles got it every time before a fight.

This was about to get ugly.

"I don't have fifty marks," Jiles said in a quiet tone.

If Larian did not know him, he would take that tone to mean Jiles was defeated. Roland did not know Jiles at all; his sneer turned into a malicious grin.

"Guess you're out of luck then."

Surprise flashed across Roland's face for a heartbeat when Jiles struck, but quickly vanished, replaced by a mask of cold concentration. Larian almost thought Jiles' gambit would work; the lithe man darted forward and to the left, kicking out with his right foot toward Roland's belly.

But the bouncer was too quick. He leapt backward, allowing Jiles' foot a pass clear of his body and causing him to pivot a bit more than he probably planned to. Then Roland advanced, both daggers descending toward Jiles' now exposed back.

The sudden move to violence rooted Larian in place. He knew he should not have been surprised, and his mind screamed at him to move, to go to Jiles' aid. But it was all he could do to watch the glittering steel streaking toward his friend's body, and cringe.

The daggers never made contact, as Jiles tucked into a roll that brought him out of Roland's reach, then popped back up onto the balls of his feet and spun to face the bouncer, his own, significantly smaller, dagger in his hand.

Whatever it was that made Larian freeze up vanished as Roland, after taking a second to assess Jiles' weapon, advanced again.

This had the potential to end badly for everyone; they

needed to end it quickly. The last thing he, and Jiles he was sure, wanted was to spill Roland's blood, or have his own spilled. Not like this, and not over something so small. Larian refused to consider whether Jiles considered the pendant big enough to kill over.

Larian licked his lips and pulled out his own dagger, then leapt forward toward Roland's back. He felt momentary surprise that the bouncer had been so careless as to leave his back exposed - hadn't Jiles said he was a really good fighter? But that did not stop him from bringing the pommel of his dagger down onto the back of his head, where it met his neck.

Roland let out a surprised grunt, then fell in a heap at Larian's feet.

Briefly, Larian worried he may have actually killed the man, he lay so still. But his chest still moved. Larian glanced at Jiles, who blinked in surprise.

"Well...that was easy," Jiles said. He stepped over and nudged Roland with his boot. The bouncer only groaned.

Then, with a shrug, Jiles squatted down and, using his dagger, sliced through the leather thong that held his grandfather's pendant around Roland's neck. He straightened, pendant clutched in his hand, and grinned triumphantly at Larian.

"Got it!"

"Great." Larian looked up and down the street, and the realization that they had just beat up and robbed a guy, in plain view of anyone who happened to be walking by or looking out a window, crashed down on him. "We need to get out of here. Now."

Jiles looked at him with his head cocked to one side, questioningly. "What are you..." Then his eyes widened and he looked down at Roland, who was beginning to stir. "Oh. Yeah, let's go."

They wasted no more time, but ran off into the night.

Five

Larian nudged his horse into motion as the column moved out. He and his fellow scouts rode in the van, as always, ahead of the command element. Behind them, the heavier cavalry led the pikeman, followed by the archers, then the supply wagons. The company on the march was impressive, but just then he was not in the mind to think on it.

He glanced at Jiles, who rode beside him. The silver pendant hung around his neck.

"Well, there's one town we'll never be able to return to again," Jiles said.

Larian nodded. No more Mirasol for them; that much was certain.

It had not taken long to convince Jiles they needed to clear out of their Inn and get back to camp as quickly as possible that night. He seemed to have put two and two together on his own during the run from the site of their scuffle with Roland to the Inn. Roland was in tight with Yohan, who was apparently chief of the underworld in Mirasol. He knew what they looked like, and there were only so many Inns in town.

They needed to clear out, and fast.

The Innkeeper probably would have protested at being roused from his bed so they could leave, so they just left his payment for the night, along with a hasty note thanking him for his hospitality and a hefty tip, in the small box he kept on the taproom bar for tips. Then they gathered up the few things they brought with them and left.

Walking, or rather jogging, back to the camp in the dark of night was difficult, and would have been even had they not been dead tired. They finally arrived around mid-morning, and passed the liberty wagon as it headed out on its first trip to Mirasol that day. They received more than a few questioning glances from their comrades in the wagon.

But no matter. They were safe. There was no way Yohan and Roland were going to go to the authorities over this. And without that, there was no way they could touch Jiles and Larian as long as they remained in camp. So that was what they did, taking duty for other men who wanted more time in town and generally keeping a low profile.

Still, Larian felt no small amount of relief when they finally packed up the camp and formed up in column for the march back to the front.

"I've been thinking about Roland," Larian said. "I feel rather bad about what we did to him."

Jiles snorted. "We defended ourselves, that's what we did. Besides, he's alive. Just got a knock on the head is all."

"Yes, but…"

"But what?"

Larian frowned, but did not answer. His thoughts were confused. On the one hand, they had robbed Roland, and that's what was eating at him. He was not a thief. Never would be a thief. And yet, he had done a thing that thieves do. So what did that make him?

But on the other hand, Roland worked for a criminal, and had probably done all manner of bad things to other people. And the pendant was rightfully Jiles'. So was it really stealing? And Roland had come at them with a knife. Two of them.

Jiles stared at Larian for a long minute, then shook his head and reached out to cuff him on the shoulder. "Lighten up, Larian. You reap what you sow, and him and Yohan reaped a whole lot of badness over the years, from what I've heard. Think of it as a little justice."

Larian nodded. "If you say so."

"I do. Besides, we're long gone now. We'll never see the likes of those two again, and good riddance."

It was probably true. But it still didn't solve the pang of Larian's conscience as they rode away to war.

Delphinus

Wind rushed past, ruffling his hair and roaring in his ears, as Piter banked right. The instruments on the control console showed what he already knew: altitude was decreasing rapidly, and there were no landing strip beacons within reception range. Not that he expected there to be any. As far as he knew, this particular world had never been colonized. He, and the huddled passengers behind him in the cargo compartment, was damned lucky the place even had a breathable atmosphere, so he wasn't about to complain. Except about the fact that the cussed cloud cover refused to break. Two thousand meters to the ground, and still there was nothing to see but pea soup in front of him, or to either side.

A fine mess they were in. Just a couple hours ago, the cruise was everything he could have wanted for his honeymoon: a veritable paradise of spectacular stellar phenomena as the SS Hilderand assumed orbit at the Lagrange point between Gamma Delphinus 6 and its third moon. The aurora there were legendary, among the most beautiful ever en-

countered, and the Hilderand's bridal suites had specially designed observation bubbles just for such an event. Making
love with his new bride beneath the awesome display was
everything they'd both dreamed it would be.

And then it all went to hell.

What happened to cripple the Hilderand, Piter couldn't say.
But once the alarms started sounding, there had been a mad
rush for the escape pods. The gravity field became erratic,
making the stampede all the more chaotic, and he found
himself, along with his bride and five others, watching helplessly as the last pod launched away from the ship. The pod
was nowhere near full, but the panicked people onboard had
been unwilling to wait even the minute longer it would have
taken Piter and the others to get there.

Alone except for those others on a deserted vessel that was
moving faster and faster into a death spiral around that third
moon, Piter forced himself to bite back tears of frustration
and despair, if only as a comfort to Shaunee. Then one of
the other men suggested they try the cargo bays, and the
group hurried further aft. In the third bay, they found a small
loading shuttle and crammed in. The only one with any flight
experience, Piter was the logical choice to fly the thing.

But twenty-five hours of flight training in a sub-orbital
wingjet does not translate well into space flight. Once Piter
got the shuttle out of the cargo bay and away from the Hilderand, it was almost as though he had no control whatsoever. He knew roll, pitch, and yaw, not orbital mechanics.
After several moments fighting with the controls, he finally
discovered a computer autopilot feature and activated it.
Things became much easier then.

He found the controls to the sensor suite and keyed in a
scan, then was unable to bite back a curse as the results came
back. The third and fourth moons had atmospheres, but

while the fourth's atmosphere was breathable, the third was little more than methane. The shuttle had just enough fuel to make it to the fourth moon, but that wasn't what evoked his curse. The escape pods from the HIlderand, programmed only to head for the nearest landing area, were all descending onto the third moon and its deadly fumes.

"My God, can't they override the programming?" asked one of the other refugees, a plump older lady with a kind smile, when Piter announced his discovery.

"I don't think so," he replied, a lump in his throat as he watched helplessly.

One by one the escape pods vanished into the moon's cloudy atmosphere, and Piter found himself thanking his lucky stars that they'd been delayed by the gravity distortions. He at once felt a twinge of guilt at the thought, but suppressed it. What else should he be thinking? What else could he think? Shaunee was sitting in the copilot's seat next to him. Tears in her eyes, she took his hand and squeezed it tight.

Then a large explosion aboard the Hilderand split the great ship into thirds, reminding Piter that there was still work to do. Refusing to think of the thousands of people who had just plunged to their doom onboard devices that were supposed to save their lives, he turned his attention to the controls and keyed in what he hoped would be a course to the fourth moon. Taking a deep breath, he hit the execute button, then settled back to wait. To his amazed relief, over the next several minutes the fourth moon got larger in the windshield.

The computer beeped. Piter tapped the controls and a dialogue window opened. "Three minutes to re-entry," he announced after reading the data on the display screen.

Immediately, the tension within the shuttle rose. They'd all been through re-entry before, but always on larger spacejets piloted by professionals. This was an altogether totally different experience. As the timer ticked down, Piter could feel the fear emanating from the others. As the one who was more or less in command at the moment, he tried his best to look calm. Glancing to his right, he could tell from the concern on her face that Shaunee wasn't fooled. He gave her hand another squeeze and she managed a thin, tense grin.

"Here we go," Piter murmured under his breath as the countdown timer reached zero. Gradually he felt Gs begin to build up from friction with the moon's atmosphere. A multi-hued cloud of plasma grew until it completely filled the windshield. The acceleration became greater. He heard the passengers groaning, and knew he was joining them: it was much more intense than on any spacejet he'd ever been aboard.

The ordeal went on for several minutes more then the acceleration began to subside, and with it the plasma cloud. When Piter was finally able to push himself forward in the pilot's chair, the radar altimeter read eight thousand meters, though all that was visible was the white-grey interior of a cloud. He took the controls again, switching off the computer guidance, and grimaced as the shuttle bucked through a pocket of turbulence.

"Looks like we're through the worst of it," he announced, and heard a half-hearted cheer from those in the rear. Of course, they knew as well as he did that their troubles were far from over. He glanced at the altimeter again: four thousand meters. Still nothing to see but the cloud.

Suddenly a large, black object appeared directly ahead. Piter barely had time to register webbed wings, talons, and a gaping maw before the shuttle struck the beast, whatever it was. The port side of the shuttle's nose buckled completely, and the windshield cracked open. Hardened plastic shards sprayed back into the cockpit, and the shuttle tumbled into a stomach-turning spin, almost completely out of control.

The roaring wind, sudden cold, screams from the passengers, and shock from the impact rendered Piter unable to react for several seconds. He'd only had the most basic instruction on stall and spin recovery in his training so far. Trying hard not to panic, he did what he remembered his instructor telling him. Reduce engine power. That had taken care of itself; the engine indications were all dead. The collision must have knocked it out. Worry about that later. Roll controls to neutral, apply yaw in the opposite direction of the spin, nose down... The altimeter continued to tick down rapidly. Not much time left. But slowly, the spin began to subside. Finally, at two thousand five hundred meters, Piter was able to return the shuttle to straight and level flight, or as close as he could get to it.

And so, a few minutes later, he found himself banking to avoid what looked from the radar returns like a large mountain range a few kilometers ahead, descending on a steep glide slope with no engine, and wondering when the hell the clouds were going to let up. Fifteen hundred meters. Still no visibility. Twelve-hundred.

Then Shaunee exclaimed, "Look!" and pointed off to the right. Or at least he thought that's what she said; it was almost impossible to hear anything aside from the wind noise. He followed her extended finger with his gaze and felt his spirits buoy considerably. Through a break in the clouds, he could see trees, or at least the alien equivalent.

Piter banked right again, and the clouds thinned noticeably. Then, a few seconds later, the shuttle slipped below the cloud ceiling and he beheld the world. Ahead, he could see rolling, forest-covered hills a thousand meters below. Off to the left, there was not a mountain range but an escarpment that stretched as far as he could see in either direction and rose up into the clouds. To the right, the hills continued for a few kilometers before appearing to smooth out. And was that a lake off in the distance?

Piter turned toward the lake, hoping to get as close to a water supply as possible before they landed. Another glance at the altimeter: five hundred meters. He needed to find a clearing or something, but there was nothing close enough to do any good. He breathed a curse under his breath.

"Hold on tight everyone," Piter shouted.

Easing the nose up to reduce the shuttle's airspeed, he looked around one last time for a better place to put down. With nothing readily apparent, he tightened the straps on the seat, then looked over at Shaunee and attempted a re-assuring smile.

The initial impact with the forest canopy sent Piter surging forward, straining against the seat straps. He felt an additional impact as someone crashed into the back of his seat, then the shuttle struck something else, and rolled to the right. Another, even more jarring impact came a half-second later, completely shattering the windshield and sending the shuttle rebounding in a totally different direction. Screams of fear and pain issued from the passengers behind. Then he felt another impact, and the seat straps tore out. Piter saw stars for a second as his forehead struck the control panel, then it all went black.

Piter had no idea how much time passed when he woke up, but it was still light outside so it couldn't have been too long. As he opened his eyes, all he could see was an amorphous blob directly ahead. He heard something, as well, but it was unintelligible. He thought he groaned, though he couldn't be sure.

He blinked his eyes a few times, and the blob slowly resolved into Shaunee's face. Concern etched into her sweet features, she was leaning over him. Her lips moved, and he realized that the sound he was hearing was her voice. What was she saying?

"...move..."

That made more sense. Obediently, he tried to sit up, and she pushed him back down again, shaking her head. But not before a wave of nausea swept over him. He almost retched, but was able to suppress the urge.

"I said don't try to move."

Piter intended to nod, but instead found himself drifting off into unconsciousness again.

When he awoke next, it was dark out, though the flickering of a nearby fire provided some illumination and warmth. The side of his body closest to the flame was somewhat comfortable, but the other...the night was extremely chilly. Suppressing a shiver, Piter raised his head to look around, inwardly grimacing in anticipation of the expected nausea. But nausea didn't come to accompany his headache, a small mercy that he appreciated more than he would have thought. Emboldened, he propped himself up on his elbows and looked around.

The scene around the fire was one of misery and controlled despair. Opposite where he lay, Piter could see the hulk of their shuttle. It was battered, barely recognizable for what it was, unusable. Two people lay side-by-side next to the carcass of the shuttle. He thought they were asleep for a moment; then he realized their chests weren't moving. He recognized the old lady with the kind smile; the other corpse was a young man, barely more than a boy, with sandy hair and a face that could have been handsome or ugly. It was hard to tell, since his face was completely caved in; he must have slammed head-first into something.

With a shudder, Piter looked away from the corpses. A quarter of the way around the fire, his gaze found his wife. Shaunee stood talking with another man, older than both she and Piter by a good ten years. The man was tall, with dark brown hair that was streaked with grey in several places and a strong face. His bearing was that of a man who knew his own worth, and that it was great. Piter took him in at a glance, but he only had eyes for Shaunee.

He chuckled inwardly at the cliche for a heartbeat, but the amusement at his own thoughts faded as he fully took in her condition.

She looked like hell. Her left eyes was black, as though she'd been in a fist-fight. Her right shoulder was also bruised, and that arm was in a makeshift sling. Her pants were torn, and he saw a scabbed-over cut on her thigh. But she stood straight and tall, or as tall as her one meter fifty-five frame could manage.

"Shaunee," he called. Or rather, tried to. All that came out was a hoarse grunt, barely audible even to his own ears. He tried again, and managed something that was at least loud enough to carry, if not entirely comprehensible.

Shaunee and the man with her looked over. Her eyes widened in surprise. Then she smiled, a broad grin of joy and relief, as she hurried around the fire to his side. She caught him in a fierce embrace. As always, he was surprised by the strength in her small limbs. Also as always, he found himself a bit aroused by it. That was awkward, considering the circumstances, but still more than a little pleasant.

"I was so worried about you," she said into his ear, punctuating her words with a kiss on his cheek.

"I'm ok," he replied. His voice was beginning to come back; he actually understood what he was trying to say.

Apparently Shaunee did as well, because she gave him another squeeze, then helped him sit up. Squatting back on her heels, she gestured toward the man she'd been talking with.

"Piter, this is Stanley Fromier."

Piter blinked in surprise and looked at the man more closely. Holy cow. Now that she'd said his name, Piter recognized him from the holo-vids. He was one of the most famous actors in the business. Hell, he'd just won Best Actor for his role in "The American King".

"It's…It's an honor to meet you," Piter managed, trying not to sound too much like a pathetic fan-man.

Stanley burst out laughing, and took Piter's hand in a solid grip.

"You saved my life, brother. I think I'm honored to have met you."

Piter looked from Stanley to the destroyed shuttle to the dead bodies next to it.

"They wouldn't agree with you."

Stanley and Shaunee looked over at the bodies as well. Shaunee frowned, her eyes returning to his with an expression of compassion and shared pain. Stanley, on the other hand, shrugged. His gaze as he looked back at Piter was direct.

"No one could have set that shuttle down in this forest smoothly. Hell, we should all be dead. But we're not, and that's due to you. When we get back, I'll thank you properly. But for now, thanks. Really."

Part of Piter's mind told him he shouldn't feel good about the job he'd done, but for whatever reason Stanley's words evoked a warm glow in his chest, and Piter smiled with a certain pride of accomplishment.

"Thanks, Mr. Fromier."

"Call me Stan."

A thought occurred to Piter.

"There were two others…?"

"They left a few hours ago to find water," Shaunee offered.

"From the lake we saw in the air?"

She nodded.

"That was several kilometers away."

"They said that's why they should head out as soon as possible. I told them they should wait until you woke up, so we could all go together, but they wouldn't listen. They took bearings off the shuttle's instruments and headed out."

Piter frowned. It would be very easy to get lost in these woods. Wait…what had she just said?

"Do you mean there's still power in the shuttle?"

Shaunee nodded.

Piter's spirits rose. "Then the rescue could still find us. We need to turn on the emergency beacon."

He tried to push himself up from his sitting position, but Shaunee prevented him from standing.

"Already done. After the other two took their bearings, we turned on the beacon and powered down everything else. So stop worrying. We've got it covered."

Piter's stomach growled, but there was no food. The shuttle had contained precious little in the way of emergency supplies: just a small first aid kit, a pack of five flares, emergency breathing equipment, and some life jackets. Shaunee and Stan had already used one of the flares to get the fire started. So there was little to do but settle in for the night. Shaunee suggested, and Piter and Stan agreed, that they should keep a watch through the night, not just to keep the fire going, but also in case the others returned and needed help.

But by morning, there was no sign of them.

On the bright side, Piter was feeling much better. He'd had

the first watch, but after that, the remainder of the night's rest had done wonders for his head. Gingerly at first, then with increasing confidence, he stood up and walked around the campsite.

In the morning light, he was able to make out details that were hidden in the night. The shuttle was crushed against the base of a tree. The trees were mammoth: trunks almost two meters in diameter, standing at least a hundred meters tall and topped by a short branches with long, wavy leaves. Several trees had been felled over a span of a few hundred meters. A few more were leaning over, bearing large gouges in their trunks. The shuttle's final descent had covered more distance than Piter realized. Looking around at the destruction, he was amazed any of them had survived the crash at all.

He and Stan spent several hours exploring the area around the camp, leaving Shaunee to tend the fire. There was little undergrowth, but despite that they never saw any sign of animal life. However, in a small clearing maybe half a kilometer from the camp, they found several bushes that were heavily laden with berries. Caution stopped Piter from immediately eating his fill. How could they know if the berries were edible or not? Thinking about it more broadly, would they be able to safely eat anything at all on this world? Despite their being able to breathe the air, the life here could very well be completely chemically different from humans. For that matter, was there even water in that lake, or just some mass of toxic chemicals? Maybe the others hadn't returned yet because they'd found out the hard way.

Piter got a sinking feeling in his belly. How long would the rescue take? Maybe they'd survived a mercifully quick death in the crash only to slowly succumb to starvation and thirst.

In the end, he and Stan decided to leave the berries. Upon

returning to the camp, they found Shaunee engaged in conversation with a man and a woman that Piter recognized from the Hilderand. They both were grubby and looked exhausted, with several visible cuts and bruises, but they seemed in fair health, all things considered.

"You made it," Stan remarked as he and Piter approached. "Any luck?"

The man, of medium height with balding black hair atop a round, chubby head, gestured to the side, where a makeshift bucket lay, filled with water. Or what looked like water.

"Not so hard getting there, but it was mostly uphill walking back. The lake looks clean enough, though. Water's tasty."

Piter looked at him askance.

"You drank it? Did you boil it first, at least?"

The man looked confused and shook his head.

"Should I have?"

Piter waved the question off and lugged the bucket over to the fire. It was too late to worry about it now, at least for them. The pair introduced themselves as Ben and Shirley, a married couple from Centauri who'd booked the cruise as a second honeymoon. Piter halfway expected them to take ill: who knew what sorts of bacteria or other bugs lived in the water on this world? But as the day wore on and dusk set in, they showed no signs of difficulties, so Piter began to think he was worrying too much. At least they had water now, however limited a supply. That was something to celebrate.

As they made preparations for the night, it struck Piter that daylight seemed to last a long time. A glance at his chronometer, set for a standard twenty-four hour earth day, confirmed it. Not that he should have been surprised. The odds of this moon having a rotation rate anything close to Earth's were minuscule at best. But it was still a bit disconcerting to be bone weary before full dark.

But sleep would have to wait a bit longer. The two bodies were starting to smell, and it wouldn't do to keep them nearby for much longer. Besides possibly attracting animals, there was also the worry of disease. So the men dug a small pit about fifty meters away from the camp proper, using makeshift tools from the shuttle scraps. Then Stan and Piter dragged the bodies over. Ben offered to help, but half-heartedly. The revulsion on his face was plain, and he actually looked a little bit green. So they waved him away and managed on their own.

Before settling in for the night, Piter went into the shuttle and switched on the instrument panel. By the indications, the beacon was still transmitting, but for how much longer? With a sigh, he powered the panel down and stepped back outside. There was nothing to do but hope. Besides, those beacon transmissions contained their coordinates, so it wasn't like the beacon had to be on continuously for someone to find them.

All the same, as he laid down next to Shaunee, he felt a surge of despair. His last thought before drifting off to sleep was certainty that they were all going to die there.

An ear-piercing, guttural roar woke Piter from a deep sleep. He sat bolt upright, and saw that the others had done the same.

"What the hell was that?" Stan asked.

Ben, who had the watch, was standing off to the side, peering out into the woods beyond the circle of firelight.

"There's something moving around out there," he said.

"No kidding," Shaunee muttered softly, so that only Piter could hear. He smirked, giving her a wink in reply.

Another roar wiped the smirk from Piter's face. Whatever that thing was, it was getting closer. Then a second roar, halfway around the camp from the first, drew every eye in that direction.

"Two of them," muttered Stan, his voice quavering as his eyes darted quickly from side to side. He inched closer to the fire, then slowly crouched and withdrew a large stick from the blaze. Burning brand in hand, he looked a bit less afraid. Piter couldn't blame him.

The two creatures got closer still, until Piter could hear their footsteps and raspy breathing, as they circled around the fire. A couple times, he thought he caught a glimpse of one of them, at the extreme edge of the firelight, but it was gone quickly. Finally, the two creatures stopped moving, over by the grave the men dug earlier. The roars became a series of snuffles, growls, and barks, and Piter could hear a rapid scuffling sound.

He gulped. "They're digging up the bodies."

Shaunee, pressing closer to him and her eyes wide with fright, shuddered.

The scuffling stopped after a few moments, and one of the creatures let out a longer, higher pitched roar. It was answered after a short moment by a number of lower pitched barks and roars, from every direction. Piter tried to count how many, but he lost track at fifteen. The new creatures quickly drew nearer, their vocalizations becoming louder by the second.

Piter bumped into something, and looked to his right to see Shirley standing close at his side. Stan was standing just as close on her other side. Without even realizing it, the small group had backed up into a cluster as close to the fire as they could. Only Ben remained apart from the rest of them, out closer to the edge of the firelight, where he'd been keeping watch.

The creatures converged on the gravesite, and it quickly became obvious from the sounds that some of the creatures were fighting each other for the meat. Barks and growls, shrieks of what Piter could only assume was frustration or pain, snapping noises: it became quite a cacophony for several long minutes. Then, silence.

"Ben, come back to the fire!" hissed Shirley.

Ben gave a start, as though he'd lost track of where he was until Shirley spoke. Then he turned around, a sheepish expression on his face, and took a step back toward the group next to the fire.

Something big and black leapt from the shadows beyond the firelight and landed on Ben's back. Piter heard himself crying out in shock, echoing the others around him, as clawed limbs dug into Ben's shoulders. Ben stumbled forward, screaming in a mixture of surprise and pain. He grasped at the claws, trying in vain to dislodge them, and fell to his knees. A head with a long muzzle and sharp teeth appeared over Ben's shoulder and bit into the side of his neck. He cried out again and grabbed at it. Then, heaving his torso forward, he pulled the creature by the head, dislodging it from himself and hurling it toward Piter and the others.

They all dove out of the way to the side, and the creature bounced past them and into the fire. It screamed as the flames ignited its flesh, and squirmed and thrashed wildly. Piter pushed himself backwards, away from the burning beast. He watched, horrified and fascinated, as the creature kicked out its last breath, scattering the burning wood in the process.

Pushing himself back to his feet, Piter turned toward Ben, and saw him resting on his hands and knees, breath coming in quick heaves. Shirley was at his side, concern etched on her face and tears streaming from her eyes as she grabbed him in a fierce embrace, heedless of the blood seeping from his wounds and staining her clothes.

Stan and Shaunee were on their feet as well, wearing stunned and terrified expressions that Piter knew he mirrored.

"What the fu…" Stan's words caught in his throat as more shadowy creatures became visible around the camp. "Oh shit," he breathed.

Piter grabbed a burning stick, tossed from the fire by the creature's thrashing, near his feet. Brandishing it like a club, he turned around, and saw more shapes on the other side of the camp as well. Frantic, he looked to the side, and saw more shapes. They were trapped.

The light from the fire, dissipated now that the fuel had been scattered, was dimming rapidly. The crouching creatures advanced steadily as the circle of firelight grew smaller. From all sides, Piter could hear raspy breathing. He could all but see salivating tongues licking over the creatures' teeth in anticipation of the kill.

"The shuttle!"

Shaunee's exclamation made Piter's head whip around toward the mangled remains of the spacecraft. She was already moving toward it, and Piter instantly understood: high ground. Keep out of their reach. The others caught on just as Piter had. Shirley and Stan hauled Ben to his feet and began moving toward the shuttle as Shaunee hauled herself atop the hulk. Piter hurried to catch up.

A roar from the side drew his eye, and his heart sank. A creature, larger than the others, was advancing toward them.

He shouted, and waved his stick at the creature. It growled, but recoiled from the flames. Piter backpedalled quickly, bumping into the others in his haste to put distance between himself and the creature. He heard Stan curse at the impact, and they all fell to the ground. In the confusion of tangled arms and legs, it took what felt like an eternity for

Piter to regain his feet.

He found himself looking into the large creature's gaping maw.

Screaming a terrified denial, Piter leaped backwards. His back struck the side of the shuttle with a solid thud, sending pain lancing through him as something dug into his lower back, near his left kidney.

Ahead of him, Stan and Shirley were only just getting to their feet, and Ben was still on his knees. The larger creature lunged forward, its teeth sinking into the flesh of Ben's ankle. He screamed, pain and terror contorting his features as the creature pulled him backwards, away from the shuttle.

Shirley screamed a throaty denial and grasped at Ben's hands, but the creature pulled him from her clutches, and she fell to the ground. Stan charged forward, striking at the creature with his own burning stick. It hit the creature on the head solidly, snapping the stick in two. The creature recoiled, dropping Ben's leg as the flames and the impact drove it back.

But two more smaller creatures darted in, jaws snapping at Stan, who had to leap backwards to avoid being bitten. They almost had him regardless, but Piter pushed himself off the side of the shuttle, biting back the agony of his protesting back, and again laid about with his burning stick.

"Help me!" cried Ben, his voice pitched high in agony and mortal terror, as the larger creature, out of Piter's reach, again bit him in the leg. Piter watched helplessly for a moment, as Ben, his fingers digging ruts in the earth as he desperately scrabbled at the dirt to try to arrest his movement, was dragged further and further away. But then it was all Piter could do to keep the two smaller creatures away from himself. Frantically striking first right, then left, he found himself backing up inexorably, barely managing to keep from being bitten.

His back struck the side of the shuttle again. It flashed through his head that this was the end.

And then he was being lifted off his feet. Hands grabbing him under the armpits from above lifted him up toward the roof of the shuttle an instant before the creatures leapt at him again. He felt a tug on his boot, and looked down to see one of the creatures dangling from it by its teeth for a moment. Then it lost its grip and Stan and Shaunee hauled him the rest of the way up.

Shirley was up there as well. Her eyes were wide, her jaw slack in an expression of mind-numbed horror and inconsolable pain. Below, Ben thrashed desperately, his screams becoming more and more shrill. The larger creature dropped him, not far from where the first creature's corpse lay, and backed away.

The smaller creatures darted in.

Stan grabbed Shirley by the shoulders and forced her head into his chest. Clutching her close, Piter heard him say, "Don't look" into her ear.

Then Ben's screams and pleas turned into a long, drawn out shriek of utmost agony as he was completely covered by the smaller creatures. Ben's death cry seemed to last forever before it finally ended in a pathetic gurgle and the sickening crunch of jaws snapping against bone.

Piter's stomach heaved, and he found himself retching: long heaves that brought up nothing from his empty stomach. It only lasted a moment, but it felt like forever before the heaves subsided. When he'd gotten control again, he slid over and held Shaunee close. She was weeping, and he realized that he was as well.

Sleep was impossible for the rest of the night, and not just because of the horror they'd witnessed. The creatures growled, roared, and barked, and tried endlessly to ascend the shuttle's hulk. One got halfway up, but Stan knocked it off with a strong kick to the muzzle. Then, after an hour or so, it began to rain, a light drizzle which quenched the last remnants of the fire, leaving them in near total darkness. Even worse, though the drizzle at first was little more than an annoyance, gradually it drenched them all, leaving them to shiver, miserable, in the darkness. It was particularly uncomfortable for Piter. The cold made his injured back stiffen up, and every position he sat or lay in was an exercise in pain.

Slowly, inexorably, the darkness began to fade, replaced by the faintest hint of twilight as the drizzle came to a stop. As that happened, the creatures' behavior began to change. While some continued to roar and scramble at the shuttle, trying to reach the survivors, several began to whinny and walk in circles. Finally, when it became light enough to see the creatures as more than just shadows moving in near-blackness, the larger creature let out a drawn-out, gurgling call, then turned and scampered away. As if on cue, the smaller ones turned their heads to the side then, in unison, turned and followed the larger one away.

Except for the five that had been whinnying. They turned away as well, but their gaits were unsteady. As they moved to follow the others, one lost its footing and collapsed to the ground. Several meters later, a second dropped. Then a third, just before the group moved out of sight. Piter could only assume the others did not make it very far before falling as well.

"Wha-" Shaunee swallowed, her gaze darting around in the gloom and her expression saying she couldn't believe what she was seeing. "What just happened?"

Piter shook his head. He was baffled as well.

It seemed too good to be true that the creatures had just left. That they weren't playing a ruse of some sort. So no one left the top of the shuttle for a long time. But finally, after it was fully light, Stan shrugged his shoulders and slid down to the shuttle's crushed nose, then jumped the rest of the down to the ground.

Piter watched, his heart in his throat, as Stan quickly circled the perimeter of the camp. Completing the circuit, Stand looked back at them and spread his hands with another shrug. Then he beckoned them to join him as he crouched down next to one of the collapsed creatures. Piter and Shaunee exchanged glances, then slid off the shuttle as well. Piter nearly fell over when he reached the ground: the landing jarred his back, sending a flare of pain running up his spine. But he managed to keep his feet and, gritting his teeth, he followed Shaunee over to Stan.

The creature didn't appear to be wounded. There didn't appear to be anything wrong with it at all, aside from the fact it was dead, and terrifying to look at, especially with drying blood still splattered all over its muzzle.

"So what killed it?" Piter said quietly.

"Hell if I know," Stan replied. "Does it matter?"

"It might."

Stan stood back up and looked off in the direction the creatures took when they left.

"Let's check the others."

The other two creatures in the camp were the same: dead, without visible wounds. A few minutes searching revealed the missing two creatures, also dead. The only difference was that it appeared one of the creatures had vomited before dying. Seeing the vomit pool, Shaunee cursed.

"It was Ben."

"Yeah, I'm sure it was, babe, but try not to think about…" Piter's words stuck in his throat as he turned his gaze from the creature to Shaunee. Her expression was serious, even grim, not repulsed. She shook her head vigorously at Piter's statement.

"No, I mean it was eating Ben that killed it."

"Huh?"

Stan cut in. "Look, maybe we shouldn't talk about this in front of…" He stopped talking abruptly and looked around in confusion. "Where's Shirley?"

Piter blinked.

"Didn't she come with us?" Shaunee asked, her voice becoming suddenly fearful again.

As they rushed back to the camp, Piter couldn't help but fear the worst. But when they arrived, Shirley was still seated atop the shuttle. Piter felt a surge of relief that died quickly as they drew nearer to her. She sat indian style, her gaze fixed on the place where Ben had died. It wasn't hard to find, as it was strewn about with chewed-on body parts, shredded clothing, and, despite the drizzle for half the night, a large amount of gore. The rest of them had made a point of not looking at it too closely, but her eyes never moved from the spot, never seemed to blink.

The three of them shared a look, then Shaunee climbed back up onto the shuttle. Stan and Piter moved away to give them some privacy.

They found the water bucket, upended and empty, not far from the shuttle.

"Well that sucks," Piter muttered.

Stan nodded. His lips pursed for a moment and he looked away, in the direction of the lake. "We're going to need more water." He paused as he looked back at Piter. "Maybe we should just go to the lake for good."

Piter shook his head. "I don't think so. T first rule when waiting for a rescue is to not move around. Stay where people are most likely to come looking. The beacon will lead the rescue here, so…" He shrugged.

Stan snorted. "This isn't the Boy Scouts, Piter. Those things are going to come back, you know. They're probably night hunters. But even if they don't come something else will. This place probably smells like a Smorgasbord."

Looking around, Piter was forced to concede Stan's last point, at least. Still, the shuttle provided a bit of shelter. And, Piter was forced to admit, being able to see a piece of civilization, however battered, was oddly comforting.

"I don't know."

Stan bent over and picked up the bucket. "We're going to need water, regardless, and it'll be safer to remain in a group. Let's just go and check out what the lake has to offer. If there's nothing promising, we can come back."

That made sense. Despite his misgivings about leaving, Piter couldn't think of any other reason to stay. And the notion of being there when the creatures returned was unappealing at best.

"Ok, let's do it."

A few minutes later, Shaunee slid down the shuttle and rejoined them. Her expression was grim.

"She's lost it. I haven't been able to get her to say a word, and she won't stop staring at…" She gestured toward Ben's scattered remains.

Piter cursed under his breath. "Well do you think you can get her to move? We're going to head to the lake, and we need to leave before those things come back."

Shaunee looked doubtful, but she nodded. "I'll try."

While she climbed back up, Stan took a moment to examine Piter's injury. Thankfully, he wasn't cut, but there was an impressive bruise that encompassed most of his left side. No wonder it hurt to move too quickly, or to twist. The women were deeply engaged in conversation when Piter lowered his shirt and looked up. Or at least, Shaunee was leaning close to Shirley and talking quietly with her. It was unclear whether Shirley was responding or not. But there was no time to worry about it. He had to trust that Shaunee would get results.

Going into the shuttle, Piter switched on the instruments again while Stan rooted through the cargo area for anything else they missed in their previous searches. Piter felt his hopes shrink, though he hadn't thought that was possible this morning. The instrument console was extremely dim; clearly the shuttle's reserve power cells were nearing the end of their capacity. He called up the transmitter status display, and was gratified to see the beacon was still functioning, though the transmit power was much reduced from the last time he checked.

Then he noticed the receiver status was flashing, and tapped to shift the display. His heart leapt. As the display shifted, it became clear an incoming transmission had come in at some point during the night. He hit the playback, but all that came through was several seconds of a barely discernible voice that was overwhelmed by static. Still, it was something, and when he switched off the console, Piter did so with much improved spirits.

Stan managed to yank a pole that had been installed as an attachment point for cargo bins from the wall. About a meter long, with a jagged break at one end where the crash had dislodged it, it would be useful as a tool or weapon. But aside from that, there was nothing else of use. Stan left. Before following him out, Piter picked up a shard of broken plastic and carved a message in the vinyl of the pilot's chair: "Went to lake. Four survivors."

Piter emerged from the shuttle and was pleased to see both ladies standing on the ground. Shirley still looked wild-eyed, but at least she was up and about. There wasn't much to bring along with them: just the bucket, the first aid kit, the flares, and Stan's pole. So without further ado, they set off in the direction of the lake.

It was a long walk, though not particularly difficult. As Ben had told them the day before, it was mostly downhill. Still, it was a good ten kilometers or more, and by the end, it was all Piter could do to put one foot in front of the other. His back throbbed with each step, and if he hadn't had Stan's pole to use as a walking stick, and Shaunee to offer him support as well, there's no way he could have stayed on his feet. But finally, they walked between the last two trees and stepped onto a field that ran down to the edge of the lake.

It was a breathtaking view. Now that they were out from beneath the forest's canopy, he could see that the clouds had parted. Gamma Delphinus, glowing white in the sky alongside its orangish companion star, was a unique enough view for Piter, who'd grown up in a single-star system. But more interesting still was the moon's mother planet, dominating the sky just above the horizon and clearly visible, even now with the stars just a bit past local noon. Combined with the highly reflective lake and a mountain range in the distance, and Piter wished fervently that he had a camera because it was an award-worthy image.

But there was no time to sit around and enjoy the view. It went without saying that the creatures would follow their trail to the lake, and they needed to find a secure place to camp. The most likely candidate was a rocky outcropping thrusting up from the lake shore a kilometer or so to their left. Piter groaned inwardly at the thought of walking that far, bad as his back hurt. But staying still, here in the open, was not an option. So he pressed on with the others.

It was very slow going with Piter barely able to walk, but

eventually they made it to the outcropping. It was about a fifty meters tall, sheer on the side facing the lake, and very steep on the others. There was only one part of the out-cropping that looked to offer a walkable path up to the top, but even that was boulder-strewn and required them to climb hand-over-hand at one point. It was perfect.

And perfectly difficult, especially for Piter with his bad back and Shaunee with her injured arm. Shirley was no help at all, just following along with a blank stare, saying nothing. So Stan was left to assist the rest of them to the top.

Even with Stan's help, the ascent was grueling for Piter, particularly the vertical ascent, short as it was. His back was bad enough, but two days without food left his stomach feeling like a huge empty cavern. By the time he reached the top, he was totally spent, and collapsed to the ground. He would have passed out if his back didn't hurt so much.

"We need to find something to eat," Stan said as he, too, flopped down onto ground.

"I don't think we can," replied Shaunee. She looked side-long at Shirley, who had settled down a short distance away and sat silently, staring out at the lake. Lowering her voice, Shaunee continued. "I think eating Ben and the other bodies poisoned those creatures, and that's what killed them."

"So?"

"So if we're poisonous to creatures here, they're probably poisonous to us also."

They were silent for a long time after that. Even if Shaunee was wrong, they couldn't exactly risk it. Piter prayed silently, forgetting for a moment that he didn't believe in God, that the static-laden voice he'd heard over the receiver was from the rescue, and that the voice's owner would arrive soon. He wasn't looking forward to starving to death.

They rested for a few minutes, then took stock of their

surroundings. There were only a few scraggly bushes and a single small tree on the outcropping. If the four of them were going to camp there, they were going to need firewood and water. Piter was in no condition to move, let alone haul heavy loads, and Shirley remained all but catatonic. So it fell on Stand and Shirley to gather what the group needed. With hardly a grumble, the two stood and made their way back down the rocks.

Watching them go, Piter felt a twinge of guilt; he should be helping. But even gathering himself to try to follow after them sent spikes of pain throughout his lower back. And, disturbingly, through his lower abdomen as well. With a groan, he laid back onto the ground and tried to relax, get some rest.

A scream roused him from a light slumber. Startled to wakefulness by the sound, he sat bolt upright, not even noticing the pain in his back, and looked around. Stan and Shaunee were nowhere to be seen. Shirley was on her feet a short distance away, still looking out at the lake. She had her hands pressed to her temples, and she screamed again, a piercing wail of pain and despair.

"Shirley," Piter began, but stopped, his breath catching in his throat, as she turned to look at him.

Shirley's eyes were wide, her face contorted with pain, but also with something else. Something…wrong, like madness. He'd never seen such an expression on a person before. Except in the holovids, and only then in tales of horror. But then, she'd been living a horror tale for the last day; they all had.

"I've lost him," she wailed, pulling at her hair with both hands. "Lost everything!"

Piter gulped. "It's going to be ok. The rescue…"

Shirley barked out a bitter laugh and turned away. More

softly, she muttered, "Rescue. What good is that?"

He tried again. "When we get out of here, you can re-build..."

"There's nothing to rebuild. It's all over."

She took a step forward, stopping on the edge of the out-cropping. Piter felt a chill going down his spine.

"Shirley, no!"

"Why not?"

Piter tried to stand, but fell over as his back spasmed. On his belly, he began to crawl over to her.

"Come back from there. You don't want to..."

"I don't want to go on."

With that, she stepped off the edge. Piter shouted her name and reached out in vain to stop her, but she was too far out of reach. She plunged out of sight, and he scrambled frantically toward the edge. Maybe she landed somewhere further down, where they could reach her. He forced himself to crawl faster. Finally, after what seemed forever, he reached the edge and looked over.

The face of the outcropping was just as sheer as it had appeared from below. There was nowhere to land except the lake, and it would be a hell of a difficult climb under the best conditions. Far down below, bobbing in the lake, he could see Shirley's body, floating face down. She wasn't moving. Deep sadness welled up within him, eclipsed a heartbeat later by anger. Anger at their predicament, at fate, and at Shirley for doing such a thing. Then anger gave way to shame at thinking ill of a woman he barely knew, whose world had just been gruesomely destroyed while she could only watch. Disgusted at himself, Piter pushed himself away from the edge and rolled over onto his back. The flare of pain as he shifted his weight only heightened his suffering.

"Piter!"

Shaunee came rushing into view, Stan just a few paces behind. Concern, near panic in fact, was etched on her face. Seeing him lying there, she rushed over and engulfed him in an embrace.

"We heard the screams. What happened?"

"Where's Shirley?" Stan added.

Piter squeezed Shaunee tightly as he replied. "She threw herself over the edge."

He heard Shaunee gasp in his ear, then begin to sob. Stan looked shocked. Walking over to the edge, he looked down for a long moment. When he turned back to them, he shook his head and squatted down next to them.

"And then there were three," Stan murmured.

There was nothing to do except say a few prayers for Shirley, then get back to work. The twin suns were getting closer to the horizon, and they definitely didn't want to be caught down in the clearing when night fell and the creatures returned. So Stan and Shaunee spent the last hours before sundown hauling up the last of the wood and water they'd gathered earlier.

As before, Piter sat, nursing his back. But it didn't get any better. In fact, his discomfort just got worse as the afternoon turned to evening. The pain spread from his lower back throughout his lower abdomen, and he began to suspect something was very wrong. Then, when he went to relieve himself and saw that his urine was bloody, he knew it for a fact.

He didn't say anything when Shaunee and Stan returned. No need to worry her any more than need be.

They waited anxiously as night fell. But by an hour or so after full dark, they'd neither heard nor seen any sign of the creatures. Eventually, even fear of the creatures' return and his increasing pain couldn't keep Piter awake, and he drifted off into a fitful slumber.

Sometime later, he became aware of loud noises nearby, and managed to open his eyes a crack. Shaunee stood close by, her back to him and a flaming stick in her hands. Stan was nowhere to be seen, but there was another light in the darkness beyond her, in the direction of the noises. That must be Stan over there. What was he doing?

Piter knew he should be alarmed about something, but what it was didn't register. He became fixated on the flames flickering atop Shaunee's stick. Mesmerized. The glow of the flame called to him, and he began to feel light, as though he was just a hair's breadth away from floating up into the sky, if only something wasn't anchoring him to the ground.

He found himself smiling, and thought with bemusement that it had been days since he'd last done that. Why? He couldn't recall.

Then darkness closed in again.

When he awoke, Shaunee was asleep beside him. Stan stood to the side, clutching his metal pole. The jagged end of the pole was covered in a greenish-grey fluid, and he had several visible cuts on his arms and shoulders.

"What happened?" Piter asked, his thoughts more clear this time around.

Stan turned to look at him, surprise flickering across his face for a moment. "They came back. One almost got to us by climbing up another's back." He glanced down at the end of his pole and smirked. "We beat them back. Blocked the path with more rocks. They shouldn't bother us again."

"That's good," Piter replied.

Stan shrugged his shoulders. "Sort of. I don't know that we'll be able to get back down again, though. I really did a number on the path." Glancing at their single bucket of water, over by the stack of firewood, he pursed his lips.

The implication wasn't lost on Piter. If they couldn't get down and back up again, they couldn't re-supply. Crap. Just then, he realized that he was parched, but he decided against asking for some of the water. Suddenly, it seemed a rare and precious thing.

The next day passed slowly.

Early in the morning, Stan and Shaunee went to inspect the path. Piter wanted to come along. He managed to convince them to help him to his feet. But after only a few steps with support from both of them, he collapsed again. His back and belly were too painful, and his legs were wobbly.

When they returned from their excursion after a long inspection, the despair in Shaunee's eyes told Piter all he needed to know before she said anything.

"Stan was right," she said.

"There's no way down?"

"He dislodged a lot of rocks and boulders last night. It's pretty impassable."

Stan shrugged noncommittally. "Maybe not completely. I can probably climb down, but getting back up...?" He spread his hands. "Difficult at best without climbing tools. Impossible with wood, or that bucket. If only we had a rope."

"So that's it then," Piter said. "We're stuck."

Stan nodded. "Afraid so."

Piter looked at Shaunee's despairing face and shared the sentiment. But He managed a smile anyway. "Don't worry, babe. The rescue would be along soon. I'm sure that's what that incoming message said."

She returned the smile and kissed him on the cheek. He could tell she didn't believe him.

There was nothing else to do but wait, hope, and conserve their strength. As morning turned to noon and then afternoon, they talked of their previous lives and their plans and hopes for the future. Or rather, Shaunee and Stan did. Piter nodded off frequently, so he only caught bits and pieces.

When he awoke in the mid-afternoon, he found himself shivering from chills, despite the fact that it was still warm out. Shaunee was seated next to him, wiping his brow with a wet scrap of cloth. What was she doing? They needed to conserve every drop! He tried to tell her that, but for some reason had trouble getting the words out. So instead he pushed the cloth away, earning a look of reproach from her.

"You've got a fever," she said, and lifted a small bottle lid, the cap to something from the first aid kit most likely to his lips. The lid was filled with water. He drank greedily, then tried to sit up, but a renewed pain in his abdomen when he flexed those muscles brought him up short, and he collapsed back onto the ground, breathing heavily.

Shaunee frowned with worry and touched his belly, sending another burst of pain running up his spine.

"His belly's hard as a rock," he heard her say to Stan, whose face turned grim.

"...Internal bleeding..." was all Piter could make out of Stan's reply before he faded out again.

It was dark when he awoke next. His vision was blurry, and it was hard to make out what was going on. There was a flickering light off to the side: the campfire most likely. Shapes moved near the fire, and he heard voices, so he knew he wasn't alone. But he couldn't manage to turn to look at them more closely, so instead he gazed up at the stars.

As he lay there, he began to get that feeling of being light again. The stars seemed to beckon, and it was almost as though they were drifting nearer to him. He felt peace, and a growing sense of joy, as one in particular grew larger and slowly began to fill his vision. Vaguely he recalled hearing about the tunnel and light that people reported from Near Death Experiences, and it occurred to him that he was dying. Strangely, he felt no fear, just a lingering sadness that he'd be leaving Shaunee alone. He tried to call out to her to say goodbye, but he couldn't hear himself speak; a growing rumble in his ears cancelled out other sounds.

But wait. There she was, standing above him, looking up at the light, and waving both of her hands over her head. You don't have to get God's attention, babe. He knows where you are. Then she looked away from the light and down at him, and he saw that she wore a joyful expression, one of relief. Seeing him awake again, she knelt down next to him and gathered him into a warm embrace.

"It's the rescue ship," she said into his ear.

He managed to return the embrace, however weakly, and smiled.

The Champion

One

When I was little I had a recurring dream where I became weightless and floated up from my bed. I would always cringe as the ceiling approached, expecting a painful impact. But instead, I simply penetrated the ceiling, then the roof above, and floated up into the night sky. I wafted on the breeze, rising higher until I passed the top of the great elm tree in our front yard.

I always felt a giddy sensation as the whole neighborhood spread out beneath me like the maps in the atlas I kept in my room. All those houses, so large and sprawling on the ground, became tiny as the models in an electric train set, making me giggle with glee.

As I floated higher, the breeze became a blowing wind that carried me swiftly away to the south. My house vanished before long, leaving me with a vague feeling of unease. But that feeling was quickly swept away by the sheer exhilaration of flight.

I zoomed through the air, rising higher and faster toward the heavens. The stars grew brighter as I left the lights of human settlements behind, filling my gaze with billions of pinpoints of light. Somewhere in the back of my mind I knew I should be getting cold as I got higher – wasn't that why tall mountains had snow on them? – but instead all I felt was a pleasant, soothing warmth flowing through my limbs, despite the fact that I was wearing only light pajamas.

Higher still I ascended and a single star, blue-white and brighter than the others, grabbed my attention. Brighter and brighter it grew, and it almost seemed to be moving toward me. Or maybe it was just that I was by then moving so quickly that it just looked that way. Regardless, the star soon filled my vision completely, and I wondered why I could still see clearly.

Then, with a great flash of blue light, the night sky disappeared and I found myself in a small, pleasant room. A fireplace crackled in the corner, lending light, heat, and the cheerful odor of wood smoke to the room. Opposite the fireplace was a small window with drapes that were decorated with airplanes and rocket ships. The window looked out onto a grassy field with a brilliant collection of stars overhead. There was a narrow door on one wall, the room's only exit besides the window.

A pair of rocking chairs with quilted cushions stood facing the fireplace, a small end table between them. Two mugs of hot steaming liquid sat on the table. The chair on the left was occupied. An old man, wispy gray hair hanging over his brows and a broad grey mustache above his lips, rocked slowly in the chair, making a soft creaking noise each time the chair leaned backward. He was dressed in an old fashioned brown tweed jacket, the kind with pads on the elbows, and matching pants. His shirt was off-white, and buttoned all the way up to the collar, where he wore a brown and yellow bow tie.

It would always take him a minute or so to notice me. When he did, he smiled the warm and welcoming smile of a man who has seen a dear old friend and gestured for me to join him in the other rocking chair. I did, and helped myself to one of the steaming cups without waiting to be asked. It was set out there for me, after all. Hot chocolate with marshmallows, my favorite.

We rocked in silence for a time, just watching the fire slowly consume the logs in the fireplace and sipping on the hot chocolate. It was so pleasant that I found myself thinking how easy it would be to just fall asleep there. How soothing it would be.

Then I would remind myself I was already asleep and this was just a dream.

And always then the old man would laugh and turn to look me in the eye. "Of course it's a dream, Timothy," he said, and winked. "But if you're going to dream, it might as well have hot chocolate in it, hmm?"

I giggled in response and he leaned over in his chair. When he came back up, he had a picture book in his hands.

"Would you like to hear a story?"

I nodded and he opened the book. It was always a different story, but with a theme I recognized and loved. The evil king captured the helpless princess. Or was it a prince, or a mystical artifact, or a book of learning? It was always different, but always a brave knight rode to the rescue, defeating the evil king and saving the day.

The stories always left me feeling excited but also confused. Who was the evil king and why could the knight never defeat him? He always rode to the rescue, but the king always returned to do more dastardly deeds.

When I asked, the old man simply shrugged and sighed a bit sadly. "He has allies," he said, knuckling his mustache softly. "As long as there are people of ill will, the king cannot be beaten forever. He can be driven off, made to lay low for a time, but never truly defeated." He perked up then and, looking back at me, cuffed me on the shoulder playfully. "Which is why we will always need brave knights to face him. We wouldn't want him to win, would we?"

I chuckled and said no, then finished off the last of my hot chocolate and set the mug down on the table.

The old man nodded and closed the book. "Well you'd best run on home now."

I did not want to go, but I knew he was right so I stood up. That was usually when I woke up in my own bed.

But one time, the old man seemed troubled. He finished the story then sat in silence, his eyes distant as he stared into the flames. After a time, I decided it was time for me to leave so I stood and went to the door. I reached my hand out to the doorknob but flinched away when the old man's voice barked out behind me.

"No!"

I turned around and found him standing up straight, no longer slouching. He was tall, taller than I thought from seeing him in the chair. His lips were drawn back in a scowl, his eyes dark with power.

He frightened me for a moment, but he must have seen it in my face because his scowl faded quickly, replaced by a gentle smile, and his eyes returned to their usual pale blue color. He stepped over to me, placed his hands on my shoulders, and gave them a gentle squeeze.

"You are not ready to go through that door," he said, his voice kind. "Maybe someday. Lord willing, perhaps you will never have to." Then he smiled more broadly, whatever care he had earlier seeming to evaporate. "Go and rest, young knight. Until we meet again."

But we never did. I never dreamed those dreams again after that night.

On occasion I would feel their lack and wonder why the dreams never returned. Of all my childhood dreams, those were the only ones I could remember with any consistency. I cannot recall any others where I knew I was dreaming either. It did not seem right that they should just stop.

But they did, and it did not take very long before the normal rigors of life brought different dreams at night, and during the day as well. I went to school, got a girlfriend, graduated, moved on to college, got a different girlfriend, changed majors three times and girlfriends five times, and finally settled into a career that I enjoyed, designing and building houses for a prominent architecture firm.

Life was good. I was successful at my job and the money flowed well. I was healthy. I got to travel a lot. I had a girl I was serious about. There was nothing to complain about and everything to be happy over.

Until that fateful day, a month before my thirtieth birthday.

Two

We had just adjourned from a meeting with the firm's biggest client. I had labored day and night for weeks to get the designs to match his exacting requirements. Each meeting before had ended in page after page of changes to make, making me wonder if I would ever see the end of it. But now he had finally signed off on the final design and given the go ahead to begin construction. Walking back to my office, it was like a weight had been lifted from my shoulders.

I keep a bottle of scotch in the bureau behind my drafting desk for just this sort of occasion. Jim, my immediate superior at the firm, and I had just poured ourselves two fingers each when Helen, my admin, stuck her head in.

"Tim, there's a Mr. Bartleby here to see you," she said. "He says he's an old friend of yours."

I blinked and looked at Helen in confusion. Bartleby? I

could not remember ever meeting a Bartleby. I opened my mouth to tell her to make an appointment for later, but Jim beat me to the punch.

"I'll get out of here so you two can catch up," he said, draining his glass in a quick gulp. "Great work, Ace."

I grimaced. Ace was sort of a nickname that senior management at the firm had for me. It made me uncomfortable, but they seemed to enjoy using it so I did not have the heart to ask them to stop.

"Thanks," I managed.

Jim clapped me on the arm and left the office, nodding to Helen as he walked past her.

She rolled her eyes at his back and smirked then looked back at me. "I'll show him in," she said and backed out of the office.

I sighed and took a quick drink, then turned and tucked the glass behind one of the pictures on top of the bureau. Whoever this Bartleby was, he had cojones to come here claiming to be my friend. He was probably some high roller with delusions of grandeur who did not want to wait to get on my schedule. Regardless, it would not do for a potential client to see me drinking in the office during working hours.

The office door swung open again while my back was turned and Helen said, "Mr. Bartleby, sir."

The door shut and I heard the man take a couple steps toward the chairs I used for receiving clients. I squared my shoulders and turned around.

"Look Mr. Bartleby, I don't know who you…"

The words caught in my throat as I beheld him. He was tall. I'm not a short guy by any measure, but he had me beat by at least two or three inches. He wore a navy blue pin-striped suit that was obviously tailor-made, probably from expensive silk, and a blue and red power tie. But it was his face that stopped me cold. Pale blue eyes below bushy grey brows. A wide grey mustache over a broad mouth that seemed to want to curl up into a smile at any moment. And wispy grey hair that hung to just below his brows.

"Hello, young knight," he said.

His voice was like a key turning in a lock. Memories rushed back, every one of those strange dreams from my childhood surging to the forefront in a rush. My jaw dropped and I stumbled backwards a step.

"Who...?" I began, then stopped and swallowed. "How...?"

The old man chuckled and set his briefcase - I had not even realized he was carrying one - onto my drafting desk. "I realize we were not properly introduced before. Bartleby," he said, "Cornelius Bartleby." He flicked open the latches of his briefcase and opened it. Reaching inside, he withdrew a weathered picture book then looked up at me. "Would you like to hear a story?"

What the hell was this? My mind raced, trying to come to terms with it. It was a joke, that was it.

"Did Jeremy put you up to this? It's not funny." Jeremy was my oldest friend. I had known him since we both were in first grade and he was the only one I had ever told about the dreams. It would be just like him to pull this kind of a prank as a pre-birthday gag.

Bartleby's eyebrows quirked upward. "I know a Jeremy, young knight, but he is eight years old in Nottingham, England."

"Don't call me that!" I snapped. "Who the hell are you?"

Bartleby shook his head slowly and cracked the book open. "Once upon a time there was a..."

I cut him off with a snarl. "Shut up! I don't want to hear your bloody story. You need to leave. Now."

Bartleby sighed and closed the book then looked up at me with earnest eyes. "I'm afraid I can't do that, Timothy. Would you mind having a seat, so I can explain?" He gestured toward the chairs on the far side of my office.

I thought of having Helen call security, but looking Bartleby in the eye gave me pause. There was no malice there, just a sort of kind warmth overlaying a deeper tension, almost like he was deathly afraid of something. I swallowed again then, against my better judgment, nodded and waved him toward the chair. He smiled slightly and turned to sit. I followed him, but paused to pick up my scotch from behind the picture. To hell with propriety, I really needed that drink just then.

"Make it fast," I said after taking a sip. "I've got an appointment in half an hour, and…"

My butt hit the chair and I lost my train of thought in shock. The glass tumbled from my hand and fell to the floor, somehow not shattering as it struck the hardwood floor with a dull thud. I did not have hardwood floors in my office.

My chair, a comfortable leather unit, was not the chair I landed in. I could feel hard slats on my back and the arms were thin, made of wood. Looking down, the rest of the chair was wooden as well. The seat was covered in a quilted cushion and I knew without looking that the legs ended on long wooden rockers.

Directly in front of me, the fire crackled and popped in the fireplace as it always did, and the narrow door stood closed off to the right.

Almost dreading to do it, I turned my head to the left, slowly. And saw Bartleby sitting in his rocking chair next to me, a twinkle in his eye and a wry smile on his lips.

"I thought a more familiar setting might make the conversation go more smoothly," he said. Gesturing toward the table between us, he added, "I'm afraid I don't have any scotch, but would you like some hot chocolate?"

Dazed, I nodded slowly. My hand trembled as I took the steaming cup closest to me on the table. My rational mind shouted out in denial of what was happening, but the rich flavor of the chocolate touching my tongue overpowered that thought. It could not be, but at the same time I could not deny that it was real.

"What is this place?" I said as I lowered the mug from my lips. I was amazed that I did not stammer.

"Between worlds," Bartleby said before taking a sip himself. "Here I meet with champions and potentials in safety and privacy, so the enemy does not know of them before they are ready for the burden."

Champions? Potentials? What was he talking about?

He must have seen the confusion on my face because he sniffed softly and spoke again. "Shakespeare was more correct than he knew. There are more things in heaven and earth than you ever dreamt of, young knight. But in the end all things serve either the Light or the Dark. The balance between the two is what keeps the universe in motion and makes life possible. But from time to time the Dark will rise up and attempt to disrupt that balance. When that happens, the Light selects a champion whose task it is to restore the universe to the way it should be." He tapped his index finger on the storybook he still held on his lap.

"The knight," I said, and he nodded. "So those storybooks are…"

"The records of the exploits of previous champions, yes." Bartleby smiled again and nodded in approval. "You are quick. Quicker than many of your brothers."

I felt my eyebrows quirking upward and shook my head. "I don't have any brothers or sisters."

"Ah but you do, young knight. Not physical siblings, to be sure. But spiritual ones." Again he tapped the storybook. I got a sinking feeling in the pit of my stomach.

"What do you mean?"

Bartleby turned his head away and focused on the flames. He sat in silence long enough that I almost stood up to wave a hand in front of his face. He chuckled softly. "That will not be necessary, young knight. I am quite well."

His words were like being punched in the gut. I felt my eyes bulging and realized I was clenching my hands on the arms of the rocking chair.

Bartleby, seemingly oblivious to the affect his words had on me, continued. "Every generation is a continuation of the struggle between Light and Dark, young knight, and can re-make the universe as it sees fit. Because of that, both sides watch the incoming generations with interest and seek out potential champions."

"Through their dreams."

Bartleby nodded again. "Think of it as a spiritual radio wave. Those who have the ability to hear and who are in-clined toward the Light join me here for instruction and guidance, so when the time comes they may make their choice knowledgeably."

"So you work for God. What are you, some kind of an-gel?"

Bartleby snorted slightly and smirked. "That is a gross simplification. But if it helps you to think in such terms, then yes. I work for God."

I groaned and leaned back in my rocking chair. This was all coming a bit too quickly. I took a deep gulp of hot chocolate and swallowed. Warmth flowed into me from the liquid, but also a feeling of well-being. My stress lessened until it was almost gone completely. Peering into the mug, I murmured, "That's good stuff."

Bartleby chuckled softly, but did not say anything.

We sat in silence while I nursed the mug and my thoughts. I expected to wake up at any moment, and even pinched myself to hurry it up. No dice; I was definitely awake. Crap.

"I suppose you're going to tell me now that I'm destined to be the brave knight from your storybooks, and that you have a mission for me."

Bartleby shook his head briskly. "There is no destiny, only choice. The last champion countered the Dark's gambit so effectively that I hoped it would be a generation or more before it tried again. That is why you haven't seen me in so long." He sighed and lowered his gaze. "I was mistaken. So I now offer the choice to take up the emblem of Light to the potentials in your generation."

What did he mean, potentials? I looked around the room again to be sure I was not imagining things. No, I was alone. Where were these others? "Umm, Mr. Bartleby…"

"Just Bartleby, please. Or Cornelius, if you prefer."

"Ok. There's no one else here," I said. "Where are the others?"

He sniffed again and stood. "They all refused."

"Wait, what?" I stammered. "They all refused? I'm the last one you approached?"

He nodded.

Great. I was the last kid picked for the ball team; it had been years since I experienced that bit of humiliation. I forgot how much it sucked. "How many others were there?" Maybe it was not as bad as I thought.

"Four hundred and fifty-eight."

Wow. Way to make a guy feel good about himself.

Without looking at me, Bartleby strode over to the door and stopped. "I once said you were not ready to pass through this door, but that you might someday. This is that day." He looked back over his shoulder at me. "Will you come?"

I looked from his face to the door. I had seen it many times before and it was always plain, painted cream with a simple chrome doorknob. Now, looking at it more closely, there were designs carved or painted into the door. Subtle designs, easy to miss: stars, planets, people, animals, flowing water. I blinked my eyes and the designs faded, only to re-appear after a moment of staring at the door. It reminded me of those annoying dot paintings that supposedly con-tained images if you just looked at them long enough, or from the right angle. I once spent most of an afternoon at a picture store in my local mall trying to pick out the image of a sailboat from one of those paintings, without success. I had no trouble this time, though.

I was already a bit spooked, but looking at that door sud-denly gave me the willies. I swallowed again. "What's in there?"

"The universe," Bartleby replied simply.

He reached into his pocket and withdrew a keychain hold-ing a number of small silver keys. He inserted one into the locking mechanism in the doorknob. There was a loud click, louder than a lock that size should have made, and the door quivered slightly in its frame, almost as if it were made of canvas and a brisk breeze had just passed over it. Bartleby took hold of the doorknob and twisted. The door came un-latched and opened smoothly inward.

Starlight streamed in through the door, and more than starlight. Awed, I found myself standing and walking over to stand next to Bartleby, my mug forgotten on the table.

There was nothing but space beyond the doorframe. And when I say space, I mean space. Stars gleamed everywhere, billions, trillions of them. A reddish nebula glowed above us and to the left. Straight ahead, a bluish cluster of stars gleamed brighter than the others. Off to the right, I could see a yellow-orange sun with a system of six planets revolving around it. Not far past it, a larger greenish-white star mothered its own small system of planets. As I watched, it became obvious that the stars were a loosely bound binary pair and were revolving slowly around each other.

"My God," I breathed and took a half-step forward, wanting to see more.

Bartleby's hand on my shoulder stopped me. "Be careful, young knight. Do not wander too far. As you are now, without my protection you would quickly perish beyond this doorway."

I nodded, not needing to ask him how. "Then why are you...?"

"If you are to become the Light's Champion, you must first see and understand the nature of the struggle, otherwise you cannot do what needs to be done."

I nodded again. "So if I go with you out there," I gestured toward the starscape beyond the door, "I'm committed."

"Only to learning," Bartleby replied. "Once you have seen all that I must show you, you will be free to accept the burden or not."

Except that he already said there was no one else to do it. I could say no, but if the forces of darkness, or whatever, were really gearing up and there was no one to stop them, it would probably mean Armageddon or something. Some choice, that. I drew a deep breath and smoothed back my hair, which must have been standing on end as jittery as I felt.

"Alright," I said. "Let's go."

From the corner of my eye I saw Bartleby smile. Then he took my hand and stepped forward, through the door.

Three

I followed, and found myself floating in the void of space, unsupported by anything except Bartleby's hand yet somehow comfortably warm and able to breath. I got a queasy feeling in the pit of my stomach, like during the drop from the top of the big hill at the start of a roller coaster. I remembered hearing the continuous feeling of being in free fall sometimes made Astronauts spacesick, and understood why. Then I found myself smirking and chuckling as I envisioned the great Knight of Light, or whatever the right title was, upchucking all over his teacher. Bartleby would not appreciate that, I suspected.

We drifted away from the door and I glanced back over my shoulder. The doorframe also floated in the void, unattached to anything. It was a very incongruous sight and I wondered where the rest of the building that housed the room was located. Then the door swung shut, apparently of its own accord, and it vanished completely.

A surge of panic filled me, and I grasped at Bartleby's arm frantically, like a man desperately trying to avoid falling off a cliff. There was no way back!

"Be calm, young knight," Bartleby said, and patted my clutching hand with his. "No harm will come to you while you remain with me."

"But…" I realized I sounded as frantic as I felt and took a deep breath, trying to will my fear away. "The door's gone."

Bartleby chuckled and swept his free hand out in front of us. "There are always more doors, young knight."

I looked forward and saw he spoke the truth. As his hand moved, dozens of doors shimmered in and out of view all around us. Like the other, they all hung in space mounted to nothing, though I had no doubt they all led somewhere.

"Whoa," I observed. Never let it be said that I am not eloquent when I have to be.

Bartleby smiled in what I assumed was amusement and looked away toward the reddish nebula.

There was no feeling of acceleration, but we began moving very quickly. The nebula grew larger and larger in my vision, and as it did its color faded and grew more dim until it vanished entirely. I blinked in confusion and looked around, wondering if perhaps we had missed it. Only when I looked behind us did I see it again, shrinking quickly in our wake and regaining its color the farther we got away from it. We must have passed directly through it, but I could not understand why I had not noticed as we did.

That question dominated my thoughts for a time and I did not realize that we were continuing to speed up until I looked around to the left and right and saw no stars. Or rather, I saw many fewer stars. Where before there were literally billions in every direction, now there were only a few scattered here and there. What had happened? I looked up, down, left, right and it was the same, just a handful of lights in the blackness of space.

Wait, it was not completely black. Off to the right and below me there was a hazy smudge of light, and another past it. Further in the distance, at the very edge of perception, other dim smudges were scattered around the sky. Now that I knew what to look for, I soon saw hundreds, if not thousands of them.

My confusion must have been showing. Or maybe he just heard my thoughts again. Regardless of why, Bartleby touched my shoulder with his free hand and said, "Look back, young knight."

I did, and was totally floored.

I had seen deep space photographs from the Hubble; who has not in this day and age? But it is one thing to see a picture of a galaxy from a telescope. It is another thing to see a galaxy with your own eyes. That is what lay behind us - our galaxy in all its glory.

My breath caught in my throat as I beheld it. The bulge in the galactic center, complete with a thin beam of light shooting up and down from its core. The bright bar of stars passing through the center and connecting the major spiral arms. The arms themselves, blue with the light of young stars except where dust clouds eclipsed the light. Globular clusters in their orbits above and below the galactic plane. It was beautiful beyond words; the Hubble pictures did not even come close to doing it justice.

Beside me, Bartleby said, "The universe in balance is a lovely thing."

I somehow found my voice. "It is."

"Light balances Dark. Stars are born, live, grow old, and die. Their light goes out, but in the explosions of their deaths, they seed the universe with the material to create new light, and new life, elsewhere. Black Holes, such as the one at the center of your galaxy," he pointed toward the bulging bar in the center of the galaxy as he spoke, "devour all matter they encounter and even light itself. Yet as they eat, they create some of the greatest lights in the observable universe." His gesture moved from the bulge to the lines of light shooting out of it. "Some of them can outshine whole galaxies by themselves. I believe you call them Quasars,"

I nodded slowly and recalled hearing about those things before in science class, during one of our introduction to astronomy lectures. But I had never thought about it the way Bartleby described, never stopped to consider the balance of forces that drove it all. Looking at it that way, it all made sense.

"It's amazing," I said.

Bartleby nodded. "And delicate. Even a small disruption in the balance can have a disastrous affect."

The galaxy began shrinking and it took me a second to realize we were moving again. We travelled faster than I could begin to conceive; part of my mind shrieked that we had to be traveling faster than the speed of light and that was impossible. But impossible or not, we were doing it, apparently. The galaxy receded into just a hazy smudge, then vanished altogether. On either side, we passed other galaxies, some larger than the Milky Way, some much smaller. All passed by in a heartbeat. We zoomed through a few too; the stars streaming past almost looked like the warp drive effect in Star Trek, but it only lasted a heartbeat before we passed through.

Finally, we slowed again as another hazy smudge grew into a collection of stars in front of us. But this was different. There was no structure like in the Milky Way. No blue of new star formation. Only the dull red glow of old stars nearing their end. The galaxy, if you could even call it that, was disjointed, devoid of dust clouds. It had a center of mass; I could see where the glowing galactic bulge should have been. But in its center there was only a globe of blackness where no stars shined and, from what I could tell, no light passed through from beyond.

"What is this?"

Four

Bartleby frowned. When he spoke, it was in a hushed voice and a tone of near infinite sadness.

"Here the Dark was victorious. This was once a thriving galaxy similar to your own. Flourishing with life and joy, glowing and singing in the night. But we were not able to counter the Dark's plans, and you see the result." He gestured toward the blackness at the center of the galaxy. "Now the Black Hole is virtually all that remains, except for a few stars that slowly burn out the last of their lives giving light and warmth to planets long dead."

I shivered with sudden terror as I looked at the destruction before me and understood its enormity. The weight of what was happening seemed to settle onto me and I gasped. "Are you saying if I...if the Champion...does not succeed, the Milky Way will become like," I gestured toward the ruined galaxy, "that?"

Bartleby gave a little start, then looked at me and shook his head. "Not all at once." He took a deep breath and turned us away from the grisly sight. "What happened here is the result of many generations of failure and neglect. No," he patted my shoulder in a comforting manner, "our battles are fought in much smaller arenas. The consequences of victory or defeat can seem small, even inconsequential. But they are real, and the cost of failure can be larger than we at first believe. In this place, though we tried to help, the Dark was victorious so often, and for so long, that the people gradually stopped fighting and surrendered, to their ultimate destruction."

I shuddered and forced down the urge to look back as we flew away. "I see."

Bartleby was silent for a few minutes as once again galaxies zoomed past us on all sides. Imperceptibly we began to slow until, as we neared a shining blue, barred spiral galaxy similar to the Milky Way, we came to a complete stop. Bartleby waved his hand through the space in front of us and a closed door shimmered into view. He withdrew his keychain from his pocket and inserted a key into the doorknob. Then he paused and looked back at me.

"I brought you here so you can see the ultimate result if the Dark is not balanced; so you can understand the choice you now have to make," he said. He waited for a moment for the words to sink in, then he turned the key in the lock, pushed the door open, and stepped inside.

I followed and found myself back in Bartleby's sitting room. The fire burned just as brightly and merrily as it had before. The mugs were still on the table, and still steaming. Even my scotch glass lay on its side on the floor in front of the fireplace. It was as though we never left.

Bartleby closed and locked the door behind me then

walked over to his rocking chair and sat down. Feeling more than a little uncertain about what was coming next, I took a moment to pick up my scotch glass before I took my own seat. We rocked for a time, the slow creaking of our chairs creating a soothing harmony with the crackling and popping from the fireplace. Gradually, the angst I felt from seeing the ruined galaxy lessened, moving to the back of my mind but not fading completely. Somehow I knew it would never go away altogether.

I was the first to break the silence. "The others all saw what you just showed me?"

Bartleby shrugged. "About half of them refused to see me at all. Only a third of the remainder agreed to join me here. Of those, a majority convinced themselves they were hallucinating and refused to go onward." He sighed and rubbed at his temples with his fingertips. "It is my fault. I should never have left your generation alone for so long. I lost so many potentials..."

His words drifted off into silence. Suddenly I felt less bitter about being the last guy called up from the bench. If that many people had not even made it this far, well, I guessed that actually made me special, in a way. I managed a half-smile as I considered that.

Bartleby chuckled, his good humor returning in time with my thoughts. "Did you ever have any doubt, young knight?" His eyes had a knowing twinkle as he turned to regard me. I got another nervous lump in my throat and made a quick shake of my head.

Bartleby smiled faintly. "It is time."

"Time?"

"To decide. Time moves on, and the champion will be needed soon."

I swallowed, forcing down another bout of nerves. "What

do I have to do?"

Bartleby returned his gaze to the fire and spoke softly. "It is always different. The Dark's machinations are never easy to spot. All I can tell you is that you will know it when you see it."

That was not very encouraging. "You've got to be kidding me. That's it? Talk about a nebulous job description!"

Bartleby shrugged his shoulders. "You will know the champion of Dark when you see him. From there, it will not be difficult to ascertain what he is planning." He sighed. "Believe me, young knight. Determining what is to be done is not the problem; doing it is."

"You do realize there are over six billion people in the world? The odds of me ever meeting…"

"You will meet," Bartleby interrupted. "You will be drawn to each other like moths to a flame. It is the nature of the conflict. There can be no victor if the champions never meet."

"Great," I growled. "I thought you were the coach here. Is that all the advice you have for me?"

"My task is to instruct and prepare the champion, not to guide his steps on the path." Bartleby inhaled deeply. "If I knew what was going to happen and where, I, or my counterpart for the Dark, could just intercede directly and shape things as I wish." He shivered as though that thought was profoundly disturbing to him. "I, and the others of my kind, are servants. Nothing more. The universe is for you and yours. Whatever becomes of it is for you to decide, not I."

Bartleby's words made sense when I considered them. I suppose it came down to the age-old question of why God allows evil in the world if He really is all powerful. I remembered asking that question myself. The answer given by a gruff old priest who happened to be sitting next to on the bus one day, Free Will, was not very satisfying. But looking at it again, in light of Bartleby's words, it made more sense.

I nodded slowly. "What happens if I say no?"

Bartleby leaned back in his chair and slowly exhaled. "Then there will be no champion of the Light in this generation, and the Dark will win by forfeit. It will fall to the next generation to resume the fight, when they are able to and assuming they are willing." He paused for a moment before adding, "But with each generation that goes by without a willing champion, the number of potentials will grow smaller until, eventually, there will be none left and the Dark will win completely."

"And then we become that galaxy you showed me."

"Eventually, yes."

I blew out a long breath. Talk about crappy choices. Another question occurred to me then. "Don't the Dark champions know what will happen in the end? Why do they do it?"

Bartleby quirked one eyebrow and snorted. "I doubt very much they are allowed to see the end results of their efforts, young knight. As to why, they do it for the same reason wicked men always do what they do: power, money, sex. Their hearts are greedy and they only see their own desires, not the affect their desires could have on others." He spread his hands in an almost helpless gesture.

I nodded again. There were always people who tried to get ahead by gaming the system or taking advantage of others. I heard stories about them every day in the news; why would people not behave the same way in the spiritual realm?

We were silent for a minute. Bartleby apparently had nothing else to say; I knew it was my time to speak. Yes or no. It was as simple as that. But at the same time, it was not simple at all. If I said yes, what was I getting myself into?

Did Bartleby really intend me to go running around fighting Dark champions in the street like some sort of demented superhero wannabe? I almost refused because of how ridiculous that would be, let alone how dangerous. But then again, he had said the arena of conflict was small, almost inconsequential. Looking at it in that light, the task did not seem like such a big deal at all. If only there was some way of knowing.

Then the image of the ruined galaxy came back into the forefront of my mind, and I realized it did not matter. Everyone else had said no. There was just me against…that. A small voice in my head whispered that would not happen just because I said no. Let the next group of guys handle it. I snarled at myself and forced the voice down. A real man does not shove responsibility onto someone else because he is afraid it might be too big. He bucks up, picks up his load, and does the best he can with it.

Or at least that was what I told myself as I stood up and turned to face Bartleby.

"Ok, I'll do it."

Bartleby nodded and stood as well. Stepping over to me, he reached out and placed his hands on my shoulders. "I am very glad to hear that." A broad smile crossed his face and his eyes seemed to shine in the firelight. Then he dipped his hand into his other pocket.

The object he withdrew flashed golden in the firelight. As he held it up before my face, I saw it was a flat golden disk hanging from a gold chain. The disk rotated around its clasp, and my breath caught in my throat. The front of the disk was inlaid in some sort of stone that caught the firelight and refracted it into a multitude of colors. The closest thing I could think to compare it to was an opal, but the shimmering colors in this stone put the best opals to shame. The stone was all of one piece and cut into the shape of a starburst. It was stunning.

Bartleby lifted the chain over my head, saying, "This is the emblem of the Light. You must never let it leave your possession. While you wear it, it will give you the ability to sense the Dark's powers and give you a measure of protection from them."

I bent my head and he draped the emblem around my neck. As the disk came to rest on my chest, I felt warmth and a sense of well-being and strength emanate from it into me. My skin tingled and I felt as though I could run a marathon at an Olympic pace. My mouth dropped open in awe, but I could not find any words to reply to Bartleby.

He apparently was used to this reaction as he smiled kindly and said, "You will become used to it." Then he raised his hands again and placed his palms on my temples. He closed his eyes and his lips moved as though he was chanting something, but no noise reached my ears.

A flash of light engulfed my vision and I felt myself falling limply from his grasp. Faintly, I heard him say, "Good luck, Sir Knight. May you be victorious."

Then it all went black.

Five

"A ce. Hey Ace!"

Jim's voice may have been enough to wake me up on its own given time, but he also shook my shoulders. Hard. I jerked awake and for a moment I could not figure out where I was. Comfortable padding beneath my backside and against my back. Bright lights. Pictures of various houses and buildings on the walls. And Jim's face hovering over mine, wearing an annoyed expression.

Then it hit me. My office.

"Were you out partying last night or something? Get up, he's going to be here soon!"

He? What was Jim talking about... Then it all came back to me. Giobald Capano, the firm's new client, had an appointment with me and Jim at eleven o'clock. What time was it? I found the clock on the wall and blinked. Ten fifty-seven. Crap.

"Sorry, Jim," I murmured as I pushed myself to my feet. My scotch glass was in my hand still. I had not slept well last night, nerves from the morning meeting and all. Between that and the scotch, I must have drifted off. That was one hell of a dream, though. I had not had a dream like that since I was a kid.

I put the scotch glass back into my bureau next to the bottle and turned back to Jim, exhaling deeply.

"You ready for this, Ace?"

I nodded. "Yeah, good to go. Let's..." As I turned, something moved beneath my shirt and I felt it thump into my chest. "What the hell," I said and reached up to my neck. And found a chain necklace there. My heart skipped a beat. It couldn't be.

But it was. I pulled the chain out of my shirt and looked at the stone-inlaid gold disk Bartleby gave me. "Holy shit," I breathed. It had really happened.

"Wow, nice," Jim said, leaning forward to look at the emblem of the Light more closely. "What is that, opal? Where did you get it?"

I cleared my throat and lowered the chain back into my shirt. "Ah, Jill," I lied. "She saw it on her trip to Sydney last week and thought I would like it."

Jim whistled softly. "That girl's a keeper, Ace." He grinned at me and then jerked his thumb toward my office door. "Let's get this show on the road."

I nodded and followed him out.

The firm's conference room was located down the hall and to the right from my office. It was a standard conference room: a long plain table with chairs to accommodate all comers and a teleconference microphone for each, a flat screen on one wall with a video camera mounted above it for showing presentations or conducting video teleconferences, a smaller table over to the side with a workstation to control the presentation, and broad windows displaying a great view of the harbor.

Jim and I were not the first to arrive. Linda and Jonas, my two direct reports, were busy putting the final touches on the room preparations: setting out glasses and pitchers of water and getting the firm's welcoming presentation up and ready on the workstation. As we walked in, Linda nodded at me and flashed a quick smile.

"All set," she said.

"That's good," I began, but stopped as voices in the hall drew my attention away.

A moment later, Lawrence O'Toole, the firm's owner and general manager, walked into the room, leading a short man in an obviously tailor-made suit. I recognized Giobald Capano from the picture in his client file, but he made a much stronger impression in person.

In his early 40s probably, he was bald, the kind of bald that spoke of frequent shaving with a straight razor more than natural hair loss, and slender, with a plain face that would go unnoticed in a crowd. He moved with an efficient ease that screamed of confidence and strength under control and he wore an easy, knowing smile on his face, as though he saw something funny that no one else in the room noticed.

I took all that in at a glance, but froze, my heart beginning to pound in my chest, as I noticed one other feature about him. His left ear was pierced by a silver earring that had what would probably pass for a black pearl embedded within it. But there was something not right about it. The pearl was more than black. It...oozed...darkness, seeming to suck in the light all around it, leaving the left side of Capano's face more shadowed than the right.

The room felt suddenly cold and I swallowed. I knew without having to ask. The Dark Champion. My new client was the Dark Champion. Son. Of. A. Bitch.

Lawrence made introductions and I remember shaking hands with Capano and saying some nicety or other. But my thoughts whirled and I was not sure what I said. How the hell was this going to work? Capano was wealthy, obviously, and had a lot of contacts in some very influential circles. Getting his account and keeping him satisfied was going to be a huge boon for the firm. Word was, he was here specifically because of my design reputation. It was flattering to hear that when Jim and Lawrence first told me of it last week. But now…

Now, Capano's desire to work with me seemed more sinister. Could he have known? No, of course not. It was a coincidence, nothing more. Like Bartleby said, we were drawn to each other. Probably had been for some time and without either of us knowing it. It made me wonder how many other people I had associated with over the years were potential champions.

That was a thought for another time. I needed to get it together and not screw up this meeting. Whether Capano and I were suppose to come to blows or not, it was not going to happen here and I certainly did not want to mess thing up with my bosses by screwing up this meeting.

So I sat down with the others and listened dutifully as Jim took over his part of the introduction presentation. Then, after a few minutes, it was my turn.

As I stood, my mind was still somewhat awhirl. Fortunately, this standard presentation was like second nature because I had given it so many times in the past. So I spoke from my script and did my part, then introduced Linda and

Jonas, who presented their curricula vitae succinctly.

Then all eyes turned to Capano.

He was silent for a moment, his lips pursed in thought. Then he smiled again and leaned forward, tapping at the tabletop with his index finger. "I have heard good things about this firm," he said. Then he directed his gaze at me and his eyebrows lifted high on his forehead. "And I very much enjoyed what you did with Kevin McIntosh's house in Miami, Mr. Williams."

I blinked. McIntosh? His was one of the first houses I helped design coming out of college, as a junior architect at a small firm in Miami. McIntosh was well off, but did not come close to matching the wealth of the people who frequented my current firm. I never actually met with him and I was not entirely sure if he would have heard my name at all since the team leader got all the design credit.

So…how did Capano know what I did on that job?

All that flashed through my head in a second. I simply smiled and nodded. "Thank you. That was a good job to break into the business from."

Capano smirked slightly and gave the briefest of nods. Then he clapped his hands and stood up abruptly. "Thank you, gentlemen. Ladies," he added with a nod toward Linda. "It will a pleasure doing business with you, I'm sure."

Lawrence and Jim exchanged glances at each other from across the table and slowly stood. I understood their confusion; usually these meetings lasted longer than this.

Lawrence cleared his throat and smiled professionally. "We are looking forward to it, Mr. Capano. I'll have Jim get in touch with your office to schedule a follow-up after his team has surveyed your current residence and completed some initial sketches ready for your review…"

Capano waved a dismissive hand at Lawrence. "Yes, yes.

That will be quite satisfactory." He flashed a smile at Lawrence, then turned his eyes toward me. "Would you give me a moment alone with Mr. Williams, please?"

Eyebrows lifted all around the table. Jim and Lawrence both turned to stare at me in confusion for a moment. The question was written all over their faces: what's going on between you and our new client, Ace? But they knew better than to ask. Lawrence simply said, "Of course," and gestured for the others to leave the room. He followed them out, only pausing to shoot me a glance that promised a grilling later before pushing the door shut.

I swallowed and looked at Capano apprehensively, but did not say anything. It was his dime; let him talk first.

He just stood there, his hands resting on the back of his chair, and looked at me with a sardonic, knowing grin. It went on like that for several moments, then he chuckled softly and walked over toward me.

"Well, well," he said. "I must say I never expected it would end up being a guy like you." His tone was amused, mocking, to match the grin on his face.

"Is that right," I stated in as even a tone as I could manage. He knew me, just as I had known him on sight. That should not have surprised me, but it did.

Capano nodded and continued his slow, even pace around the table to my chair. "You needn't worry...Ace," he said, putting a little extra mockery into my nickname as he spoke it. "I won't pull the account from your firm over this. I see no reason we can't get along professionally." He reached the chair next to mine and bent over so that his head was level with me. He reached out and gave my shoulder a companionable squeeze that was perhaps just a little bit too strong. "Do not cross me, Ace. I am not a man to be trifled with." He smiled then, a broad smile that could almost be mistaken for one of friendship except for the naked malice in his eyes. "Are we clear?"

At his touch, a shiver of fear went up my spine. His grasp was cold and felt somehow unclean. It was also very strong; clearly he worked out a lot, which was more than I could claim. But I had interacted with pompous, fit guys who tried to be intimidating before. Capano, though…looking into his eyes I could tell he meant every word he was saying.

I pulled away from his grasp and said, "We're clear." I managed to impress myself by keeping my voice level.

Capano nodded once then turned and walked briskly from the room. I saw him nod to someone out in the hallway, Lawrence or Jim no doubt, before the door swung shut behind him.

As the door shut, tension flooded out of me in a rush. I slumped forward and rested my head in my hands, exhaling forcefully. "Holy crap," I muttered to myself.

Six

This was going to get ugly.

But then, what did I expect when I agreed to do it? A walk in the park to the music of harps?

I shook my head and took a deep breath, then forced myself to my feet and smoothed my hair. This was not the time to lose it.

Lawrence and Jim were waiting in the hallway as I stepped out of the conference room, concern and curiosity etched on their faces.

"Ace," Jim said. "What was that? Is…"

I interrupted him with the quickest lie I could think of. "He just wanted to ask a question about the McIntosh house. How we could apply some of the designs into his. That's all. No problem."

Eyebrows quirked upward again and I could tell neither man was satisfied with my explanation, but I did not give them time to question me further.

"Excuse me, guys. I'm meeting Jill for lunch in twenty minutes," I said. Which was totally true, but also a cop-out. But it worked; they did not accost me further as I walked away.

I took a minute to grab my car keys from my office and hurried out. The firm is on the tenth floor of a commercial high rise near the waterfront. I had a reserved parking spot in the garage beneath the building - a nice perk. As I drove into the late morning traffic, I asked myself where I thought I was going. I was supposed to meet Jill as Bernardo's, a nice little bistro on the outskirts of downtown, but the morning's events had left me without an appetite. Well, that was not entirely true. I was hungry all right, but for answers, not food.

I tapped the bluetooth control on my steering wheel and said, "Call Jill." Jill answered on the second ring.

"Hi handsome."

"Hey babe. I'm sorry but I'm not going to make lunch. Something's come up here." As I spoke, I turned a corner and headed in the direction of the public library. What I needed was there. Probably.

"Oh," Jill responded. "That's funny, I was about to call and cancel on you, too. Mario asked me to take over one of Dave's projects since he's in the hospital, and I'm swamped."

"What happened to Dave?"

"Appendicitis."

"That sucks. I'll see you tonight and we'll talk about it then. Try not to pull your hair out."

"Yeah right."

She hung up as I pulled into the library's mostly empty

parking lot. It had been a while since I spent any time in a library. These days, I did my research online. But it would probably be a good idea to not allow this research to be traced back to my home internet access. The library seemed a good, anonymous place.

As I expected, they had a number of public internet access terminals in the back corner of the main reading area. The fee to use them was minimal, not that I cared either way, and the signup procedure simplicity in itself. Within minutes, I was ensconced at a terminal.

Giobald Capano. His name brought up several pages of search results. I was surprised to find one of the first was a Wikipedia article. That seemed a bit excessively pompous. It was good for me, though. I quickly learned more than I ever wanted to know about the man.

He started out as a busboy in Palermo and gradually worked his way into some of the local artsy circles. Somehow he convinced people to lend him money to buy a small building, which he refurbished into upscale apartments. From there he acquired numerous other real estate holdings and branched out into venture capital. He invested in numerous startups and had become known as a savvy commodities trader as well. He hobnobbed with heads of state and celebrities of all kinds and was on the Boards of several big name charities. And as if that were not enough, he spoke Italian, English, German, Japanese, and Chinese, was a black-belt in Aikido, played the violin, and was dating a supermodel.

Not too intimidating. Not at all.

On paper, at least, he seemed like a standup guy, a pillar of the community, and all that good stuff. There had to be more. He was not the Dark champion because of his good deeds.

I finally found it on the fifth page of search results. A story on a small news blog in Georgia. Two years ago, a local man had been hiking in the hills and stumbled upon a ramshackle old cabin in a sheltered valley. It was falling apart, but inside the man found an intact lockbox that held a number of old documents. He went on to sell it to a collector: Giobald Capano. There was a picture of the two of them shaking hands in front of a local bank, where they had apparently sealed the deal.

It was nothing, really. A tiny story about a very minor event. Besides historians, who cares, really, about a bunch of old papers? Yet the story leapt out at me. Even after I paged back to the search engine results list, that link among all the other seemed to pulsate, to glow more than the rest of the monitor's LCD display. There was no rational way to know it, but I did - this was it. Something about this little deal - well really not so little - Capano had paid the man five million dollars - was central to what has happening with Capano and me.

I printed out that article and went back to the office, stopping briefly for a Hardees hamburger.

I somehow managed to fend off the worst of Jim and Lawrence's questions with explanations that seemed lame to me but that apparently satisfied them. The rest of the afternoon, I tried in vain to get started on the design for Capano's house. I tasked Linda and Jonas with some of the basic designs and then sat at my desk trying to work on the overall plan. But the knowledge of who he was, the puzzle of the Georgia document purchase, and general angst over the entire situation left me unable to concentrate. I kept going over it all in my mind, but got nowhere.

Finally I left for home, feeling frustrated and confused.

I lived about twenty minutes from work, in the tenth floor

corner unit in a condo building on the outskirts of town. Not the swankiest place in town, but it had a nice view of the downtown skyline and the rent was affordable. I had lived there for four years, ever since I moved up from Miami, and did not see the point in moving just because I got promoted to team leader under Jim last year.

My building had an offset parking garage with assigned spots, but I did not mind the short walk to the tenants' entrance. A little fresh air helped clear my head after a long day. The ride up the elevator was quick, and before long I was home, sweet home.

I fixed myself a scotch and sat in a stuffed chair facing the window. There I let my thoughts wander. What was so special about that find in Georgia? And how could it possibly pertain to the battle Bartleby described? I could not wrap my head around it. It's not like we were talking about a weapon, or some monumental document that would undercut people's belief systems or reveal that the entire economy was a lie, sending it crashing to the ground, never to return. It was mundane.

But apparently it was not that mundane, otherwise Capano would not have paid five million for it.

Crap.

We were supposed to go by Capano's current residence tomorrow. His assistant was going to show us some of his favorite pieces of art, furniture, and what have you that he wanted to accentuate in his new house. That might sound strange, but I had seen wealthy clients ask for more ludicrous things than that. One guy in Miami wanted an entire bedroom built for his prize-winning Chihuahua. He spent almost six figures on that room alone. So I had learned not to be surprised by a client's request.

But Capano inviting us - inviting me - into his home surprised me. It was almost like he was flaunting himself, daring me to take a shot at him. But that was silly. Why do that after warning me off in the conference room?

Jill arrived just then, breaking my chain of thought with, "Hey handsome," spoken in her melodious alto.

I stood up to greet her and we set about cooking dinner. Jill had a place across town, a nice little townhouse, but these days she spent more time here than there. I had not thought about it too much, or rather I had avoided thinking about it, but we were getting to the point where we would have to talk about the next step soon.

But not tonight. Tonight was for grilled filets, garlic mashed potatoes, and greens.

We spent a pleasant evening together. But I continued to be distracted by my new task and found myself making mono-syllabic answers to Jill's remarks from time to time. She noticed, and asked what was wrong. I managed to satisfy her with an explanation about a stressful day at work, which was true. But I could tell she wanted to know more. Maybe later, when I figured out how to tell her without making her call for the men in white coats with straightjackets.

Jill begged off spending the night; she had an early morning at work tomorrow. We said goodnight at around ten-thirty and I hit the sack.

And was unable to get to sleep. I tossed and turned for what felt like forever, my mind awhirl still. What was I going to do? What was I supposed to do?

Fatigue will win out over mental distress, though. I eventually drifted off, and was not at all surprised to find myself in Bartleby's sitting room again. As before, the old man was rocking in his chair, making soft creaking noises. Two steaming mugs sat on the table again as well.

I wasted no time, but walked over and stood in front of

Bartleby with my hands on my hips. "Ok, Bartleby, you want to tell me what the hell I'm supposed to do here?"

Seven

One eyebrow twitched upward on the old man's brow and he gestured toward my rocking chair. "Why don't you tell me about it," he replied, his voice kind and patient.

With a sigh, I sat down and grabbed up my mug. In between sips of hot chocolate, I related my encounter with Capano in the conference room and what I had learned about him from my research. As I reached the end of my tale, Bartleby blew out a long breath, billowing the whiskers of his mustache slightly.

"Well," he said, "I can't say I've heard of the two champions meeting so quickly before." He rubbed at his nose with his index finger for a moment, then mused, "It's almost as though he was looking for you specifically."

"I thought that same thing," I replied. "But that's not possible, is it?"

Bartleby cleared his throat. "Normally, no. But your generation, as I stated before, is different. My presence masks the potentials from the Dark's notice. In your case…" He sighed and hung his head. "In your case, I thought there would not be need for your generation, so I left you alone. Apparently in my absence, the Dark guide learned of your and the other potentials' identities. As they declined the task, one by one, it was probably just process of elimination to reach you."

"Well that's great," I spat. "So he's probably ready for me, whatever I do."

"That is possible."

I growled and took a longer drink from my mug.

"Now as to the object in question," Bartleby said, as though his last revelation was no big deal at all. "You must understand that our conflicts are not normally large."

"You said that before."

Bartleby nodded. "It may be that this object has a special significance for a few people, or maybe just one. Its presence, or lack, may be all that prevents or causes those people from going over to the Dark."

"How?"

"I cannot say without knowing more about the object. And really it is immaterial. The important part is the impact on the people around it." He looked at me with narrowed, shrewd eyes and pointed his index finger at me. "Remember, sir knight, even a single person's actions can have ripple effects that resonate long after he is gone and can alter the world greatly, for good or ill."

"Great," I said. "So what am I supposed to…"

"When you see the object in question," Bartleby interrupted, "you will know what to do."

"That's not terribly helpful."

"It is the best I can do. Good luck, Timothy."

I would have retorted harshly, but the sitting room faded away in favor of a scene so bizarre it had to be another dream. I recall resisting for a heartbeat, but then the dream took me and I slept, oblivious to the fact that I was dreaming, until my alarm clock woke me at my usual time the next morning.

The morning routine went as normal. I got into the office at 8:30 and sat down at my drafting table. Linda and Jonas had left their initial drawings from the day before on my desk when they left, but I was too distracted yesterday to do a good job of reviewing them. I spent twenty minutes looking the drawings over then pushed them away. I thought of several ways to improve on the drawings off the top of my head, but it was a good start overall.

At 9:30, after my morning meeting with them, we found Jim in front of Lawrence's office. The two men were exchanging quiet words, stopping quickly when the three of us arrived. Jim glanced at us - at me - then looked back at Lawrence and nodded. The two exchanged a meaningful look and Lawrence went back into his office.

"Ready to go?" Jim asked as he turned back to face us, his normal cheerful grin on his face.

I nodded and Jim led us down the corridor to the elevator.

The firm kept a van down in the garage for these sorts of excursions. The four of us piled in after loading our notebooks and other equipment into the back, then Jim got behind the wheel and drove us away. It was a forty-five minute drive to Capano's house. Nestled in the hills west of town, it looked over the countryside from an unobstructed vantage point. The view was amazing.

"Why the hell is he moving?" Linda breathed as we got out of the car.

"He bought some beachfront property," I replied in annoyance. She should have known that; it was in the client information packet we had all received when we were tapped for his account. But this was not the time or place to poke her for not doing her homework.

Capano's house, his estate really, had a huge set of arched double doors, carved simply from dark, reddish wood with narrow panes of glass inlaid so those within could see callers. They swung open as we approached and a tall man, dark of skin and hair, stepped out to greet us. He was well dressed in a simple but elegant black suit and carried himself with erect poise that exuded confidence and professionalism.

"Good morning," he said with a shallow inclination of his head to us, "I am Jasper, Mr. Capano's personal assistant. You are from the architecture firm, yes?"

Jim responded in the affirmative and introduced us. Jasper acknowledged each of us with cool politeness, but I could tell he really was not all that interested. We were a task on the checklist for the day, nothing more.

"Mr. Capano regrets that he cannot be here to liaise with you himself, but pressing business prompted him to leave the country last night. You know how it is." He sniffed softly and flicked his eyes over us in a way that said, 'You don't know how it is, you peons. And you know that I know it.' Then after a heartbeat's pause, he said, "If you will follow me?" and walked back into the building.

"Abrupt, isn't he?" Jonas observed, earning himself a sharp look from Jim.

We followed him inside and Jasper proceeded to show us around Capano's house. It was, of course, huge and sprawling. But I was not prepared for its elegant simplicity and the highly tasteful way he decorated. I am not sure why; perhaps I thought the Dark champion would go for torture devices and pitchforks, or maybe decor along the lines of Montana's house in Scarface, gaudy and in poor taste. A silly thing to think, but that's how it was.

The dwelling revealed a man that I could probably come to like. His book collection was extensive and eclectic, as was the art on his walls. His furniture was plain, unadorned, but of the highest quality. He was a sports fan; one room was set aside as a home theater, which was lined with pictures of various famous sports figures and team emblems, his favorites I assumed. I spied a few of my personal sports heroes up there as well. The overall impression was that of a man who appreciated the best things in life, but did not care about flamboyance. Again, not what I expected.

It took a good hour and a half to complete the walk-through. There were a number of items Capano would want just so in his new residence. Pieces of art that needed to have custom-created displays, an annoying feature of the kitchen that he wanted removed, things along those lines. None would be particularly taxing, but taken together they required a lot of work to get it right. Which is why our firm's fees were so high.

From a professional standpoint, it was a productive trip. But by the end of the walkthrough, I began to get frustrated. The house said a lot about Capano, but there was nothing that gave even a hint of what his Dark plans might be.

Then I saw it. A small picture frame in his sitting room, mounted near a panoramic window. Within the frame was a yellowing page, not much larger than a sheet of letter-sized paper. It seemed to glow with an inner radiance that drew me, an almost magnetic pull to walk over and look at it.

"What is this?" I asked.

Jasper had already turned to leave the room but stopped and turned back to me, annoyance on his face. I suppose I had disturbed his carefully designed schedule for the walk-through or something. His lips pursed and he shrugged slightly. "Mr. Capano has a fondness for antiques."

Really. I had not noticed from the rest of his decor. I kept that thought to myself. "It looks like the map of a coastline somewhere."

Jasper nodded. "The oldest known map of the Carolina coast. Mr. Capano bought it a few years ago. Now, if there are no other questions here, you really must see…"

His words faded from my hearing as I focused in on the map. It was old, yellowing, faded, fraying at the edges, and torn. One place in particular was distinctively marked as though it was important for some reason, but the writing there was so faded I could not make it out. If only…

"Ace, come on!" Jim tugged on my arm, breaking me from my contemplation.

I jumped, startled, and gave him a sheepish smile. "Sorry."

He looked askance at me and opened his mouth to speak again, but I stepped past him and out of the room, hurrying to catch up with Jasper and the other two in the hallway. It was an effort; I still felt the magnetic attraction to that map. I knew for certain that it was the document Capano had purchased from the man in Georgia. That meant it was important, somehow. I needed to find out why.

Back at the office, I set my team to work then went to my desk to ponder. Capano's demands for his house were exacting. But then, he was going to spend I did not want to think about how many millions of dollars for a brand new house at the beach, so why should he not get exactly what he wanted?

I blinked and leaned forward in my office chair, my eyes widening as it hit me.

A brand new beach house.

Eight

With a strangled cry, I turned to my bureau, pulled out Capano's client information packet, and leafed through it hurriedly. It was here. It had to be. And there it was - the address of Capano's new house, complete with overhead shots Jim or Lawrence probably obtained from Google Earth. But they were zoomed in too tight. I swallowed and turned to my computer then entered the address into Google Maps and waited for the page to update. It was zoomed in close, so I clicked out a few times.

I leaned back in my chair and stared at the screen for a moment. A chill went down my spine and I realized I was getting goosebumps, but not from the cold. The map showed the same coastline as the map on Capano's wall. And his property was in the exact spot that had been marked as important on his map. That could not be a coincidence.

What was I going to do? No sooner had I asked myself

that question than the answer came to me. It was obvious; the only problem was getting Jim to agree to it.

It was easier than I thought it would be.

My flight departed at 7 am. I almost missed my connection in Charlotte because of weather in the mid-west, but it worked out and I landed in Hilton Head, South Carolina at 2 o'clock in the afternoon.

The humidity was the first thing to hit me as I walked out of the airport. It had been years since I last came below the Mason Dixon line; I immediately began to sweat. A little voice in the back of my head asked me why the hell I had come down to this furnace of a place, and why I had worn slacks and long sleeves instead of a t-shirt and shorts. But I did not waste time standing around. Instead, I strode over to my rental car and cranked up the air conditioning.

I checked into a small timeshare condo a few blocks back from the beach. I was not planning to stay long. Just long enough to survey Capano's new lot, take some pictures, and get a feel for the local utility arrangements so we would have a better starting point for the design. At least that was what I told Jim. He ate it up and wasted no time in having the firm fork over money for the trip.

I did not eat on the plane, so I took a few minutes to wolf down a quick lunch, then hit the road.

Capano's lot was not strictly speaking an ocean view. Situated at the southern tip of the island, it actually looked out into the Calibogue Sound between Hilton Head and Daufuskie Island. But there was a beach, his house would be right on it, and if he turned his head to the left he could see the actual ocean, so I supposed it was close enough.

I pulled to a stop a few houses down from his lot and got out of the car, camera in hand. The street was wooded, with expensive-looking houses, some more palaces than houses and several probably condo-ized from the look of them, everywhere I looked. Looking back and forth along the street, though, I frowned. There was something not right about this.

As I walked the few hundred feet from my car to Capano's lot, I mulled over where that feeling came from. Then it hit me.

Capano preferred simple elegance. That was obvious from his manner of dress and his house in the hills. This place was...too cluttered, almost. The houses, big as they were, were too close together. The trees growing everywhere made it the outdoors seem enclosed. The whole block did not suit Capano at all.

And then I saw his new property. It was long and narrow, backing up to the beach. An older house stood about a third of the way back on the lot. It was not as large as its neighbors, though it was by no means small. Brown wood siding, a screened in porch in front, an detached two-car garage: it was definitely not to his taste.

Which is why we was tearing it down to build a new house, a voice in the back of my head said.

Maybe, but I was certain he bought this place was because of that map, not the lot itself.

I walked up the driveway, noticing recent survey markings along the lot's boundaries, and snapped off a few pictures. Jim would crucify me if I did not come back with something usable for the design. And truth be told, it was important to know the lay of the land if I wanted the new design to be the best it could be.

But I was not really there for architecture.

I walked past the house and into the back yard, then blinked in surprise. A front-end loader with a backhoe attachment and a little bulldozer were parked there. It was a little early to start razing the lot, wasn't it?

Then I saw the hole.

It was about fifteen feet across, twenty feet long, and five to ten feet deep. Capano had clearly used the construction equipment to dig it out. Why? I walked to the edge of the hole and peered down.

My breath caught. There in the center of the hole was a carved statue of a woman. She sat on a rock, nursing a baby she held in her arms. Around both the baby's and mother's heads were halos. I had seen that image many times before. But never had I seen a rendition that actually glowed. This one did.

"The Madonna and child."

The masculine voice surprised me, making me jump and turn around in a rush.

I should not have been surprised to see Capano emerging from the back door of his house, but I was. He wore loose-fitting khakis and a blue polo shirt, but he walked with a quiet dignity that made his outfit seem formal.

"I knew you would come," he said, stepping from the back porch to the yard. "It was inevitable."

"It was necessary if we want to make the new house fit with its surroundings," I replied, my tongue thick in my mouth. I managed not to stammer, despite the anxiety, slowly growing into outright fear, that I felt.

Capano snorted. "Let's not play each other for fools, Mr. Williams. We both know why you are here."

I took a step back, maintaining distance between us as he moved to the edge of the hole. "I guess that makes one of us," I said, gesturing toward the statue.

Capano's eyes flicked down to it and he smirked. "Probably one of the oldest European artifacts in this area," he said. "Made by the French Huguenots who settled Port Royall in 1562. Or maybe the Spanish explorers in 1526, though

I doubt they would have taken the time to carve statues on their journey."

"I imagine it's worth a bit of money. Is that why you bought this place?"

Again Capano snorted. "It is, but not that much. I spent far more on this lot than I could ever hope to make selling that thing." He said thing in a strange tone, almost as though he found the statue distasteful. Maybe he was one of those guys who does not approve of breastfeeding, but I doubted it. It went deeper than that.

"I guess you really wanted a beach house then. Can't say I blame you. It's nice around here."

"It is. But my house in Cancún is better."

I frowned but did not reply. I took a moment to look back down at the statue. The soft glow it gave off was clearly visible, even in the direct sunlight. Also, it seemed to…tug…on me. In almost the same way the map on Capano's wall had. This statue was important.

"Why do you want the statue?"

Capano cocked his head to the side, like a bird, and looked at me in silence for a moment. Then he shrugged. "I really do not."

"Then why…?"

"Are you a man of faith, Mr. Williams?"

I shrugged. "Haven't really thought about it."

Capano's eyebrow twitched upwards. Surprise? His voice was level as always when he spoke. "Faith is a strange thing. The people who carved that," he gestured to the statue again, "had faith in what it stood for."

"Ok," I said slowly. Where was he going with this?

Capano smirked and shook his head slightly. "You do not understand. No matter." He sighed deeply and looked at me with flat eyes. "I warned you not to cross me, Ace." His right hand slipped behind his back and emerged holding a semi-automatic handgun. He pointed it at me. "I'm sorry it had to come to this."

Despite the summer heat, I suddenly felt cold. I backed up another step and raised my hands. "You're going to shoot me? Here in broad daylight?"

Capano shrugged. "Why not? That house is vacant," he pointed with his free hand toward the house to his left, "Foreclosure proceedings, or so I hear. That one," he pointed to the right, "is a vacation rental, but no one's in there until next week. And the old lady across the street is hard of hearing." His smirk widened into a wicked grin. "Couldn't resist following my little trail of breadcrumbs, could you?" He raised his voice a bit. "Boys!"

From the shadows behind the garage came two burly men. One was black, the other asian, but there was essentially no difference between them. They had no necks, their biceps were almost as big around as my thighs, and they wore murderous scowls beneath dead eyes. Both wore dark slacks and collared white shirts that were open at the neck, and handguns in shoulder holsters. One of them carried a canvas sack, the other a length of rope.

Nine

O h crap," I muttered, and turned to run.

And was stopped within a step by the report of Capano's gun being fired and a piece of turf kicking up just in front of me.

"Next one goes in your chest," Capano said. "Don't move." He chuckled viciously. "It'll hurt less."

The two guys grabbed me. I tried to struggle, but I almost never work out and I certainly never learned how to fight; I was like putty in their hands. Inside of a minute, they tied me hand and foot, pulled the canvas bag over my head, and pulled the drawstring tight. Then they picked me up by my shoulders and feet.

I began swinging back and forth, and I heard one of the men counting.

"One."

What the…?

"Two."

Oh crap.

"Three."

I opened my mouth to speak, but all the came out was a short scream as they released me and I fell somewhere; into the hole I thought. I landed with a soft splat; the bottom was more mud than dirt. Gotta love the high water table in the coastal south.

The breath left my lungs and I spent a moment coughing and gasping. The bag over my head did not help matters at all. It made breathing very difficult and was already unbearably hot. This was bad. Very bad.

"Enjoy your stay," Capano said from above me. Then he muttered something more quietly to the two men.

A moment later, I heard a loud engine start up - probably one of the digging machines in the yard. Then rocks, pebbles, and loose dirt fell on me and I felt a surge of dread. They were filling in the hole, with me in it! Dread turned to terror as I contemplated being buried alive.

I rolled away from the area where the dirt came down, but only managed to roll about three quarters of a turn before my shoulder struck something solid. The statue. But why was it still here? I thought getting it was the whole point?

The sounds from the digger grew louder again and I heard and felt another scoop of dirt fall into the hole. There would be time enough to figure out what was going on later. Now I needed to get the hell out of there. Somehow.

I squirmed around, trying in vain to get to my feet. All I managed to do was slam my cheek into the corner of the statue's base. I saw stars and felt a stabbing pain, then wetness as I began to bleed. Son of a…

Thoughts of complaint vanished as I realized what had just

happened. Another pile of dirt fell down as I pushed with my feet, slowly maneuvering my hands to the statue's corner. I traced the edge with my fingers and felt a surge of hope. It was rough, almost sharp. Praying silently that I would have enough time, I squirmed around until I had the rope binding my hands running along the edge, then I started rubbing it back and forth.

It took forever. Or at least it seemed that way. But when you're tied up, blind in a pit and a thug is continually raining dirt and rocks down on you, time can be a little hard to judge. The side of the pit I'd just rolled away from was beginning to fill; my legs and lower abdomen were now covered in dirt. The weight of the earth was substantial, but I could still move, for now.

I was just beginning to think that by the time I got the rope cut I'd be buried anyway when the rope snapped. I stopped in surprised disbelief. It had worked!

Another pile of dirt falling down was all the encouragement I needed to get moving. I yanked my hands free of the rope and pulled the bag off of my head. Daylight made me cringe and clench my eyes shut, but that discomfort was nothing compared with the sheer bliss of fresh, cool air.

It says something that the South Carolina summer heat was cooler than the inside of that bag. I was tempted to sit there and just enjoy breathing, but I heard the digger coming back. There was no time to waste. I hauled myself out from under the dirt and set to work on the rope binding my feet. It took a lot less time to get the knot untied than it had to cut through the rope. By the time the thug dumped the next load of dirt, I was free and clambering to my feet.

The hole was about a third full, the dumped dirt making a sort of ramp up to one side, where the thug had been dumping it, no doubt. The statue was at my feet, but there was nothing else close to hand. I pondered for a moment, then hefted it. It was about two feet tall, but not terribly heavy, maybe thirty pounds. Part of me wanted to leave it behind and just go, but I knew the statue was the key to this whole thing. Plus, it might make a nice cudgel to hit the thugs with.

I saw the little bulldozer backing up from the lip of the hole. Its scoop was raised, so there was a good chance the thug at the wheel could not see me. I scrambled up the ramp of dirt, having to claw and dig my way up. By the time I reached the top and peeked above the rim of the hole, the bulldozer was scooping up another load of dirt. The asian guy was at the wheel alone. I glanced back around quickly and could not see the other thug. I ducked back down beneath the lip of the rim as the thug turned the bulldozer back toward the hole.

I waited, the bulldozer's noise growing louder by the second. Then the scoop appeared, moving forward above the lip of the hole. It stopped moving and I surged upward, pulling myself out of the hole completely. The scoop tipped forward, dumping out its load dirt, as I reached my feet.

The thug's eyes widened in surprise. He took his hands from the wheel, his right dipping toward his gun.

I had only seconds to act. I bounded forward, raising the statue in both hands as I leapt up onto the step beside the bulldozer driver's seat. The thug's eyes grew even wider as I brought the statue down full force.

CRACK! The statue struck the thug in the left shoulder. He bellowed and went over to the right, still in his seat. I struck again. This time the statue struck his head. His body went limp and he fell from the driver's seat, landing on the turf beside the bulldozer with a dull thud.

I stood there, amazed that my gambit had worked and gasping for breath, for several moments before I remembered the second thug. I was a sitting duck if he was lurking around somewhere.

But he was nowhere to be seen when I turned around to look. I did not stop to question where he went, I just ran as fast as I could back to my car.

Ten

Back at my room, I stripped off my clothes and took a long, cold shower, then got dressed in a clean shirt and khakis and drank several glasses of water. Once I was feeling human again, I sat down at the table where I had placed the statue and examined it.

Maybe it was well crafted back when it was made, but now it did not look like much. It was weathered, eroded by dozens of decades exposed to the elements. All the same, it was beautiful in its simple depiction of a woman's love for her child. I sniffed softly. Of course, this was not supposed to be just any child, or just any woman. But there were countless renditions of Madonna and Child in the world. Why was this one so important?

I turned the statue around on the table. To my eye, it still gave off a soft glow. But as I looked more closely, I could see the glow was not uniform. One place near the center of the statue, just below where Mary cradled the baby Jesus, glowed more strongly than the rest. I leaned forward and gasped. There, barely visible against the rest of the stone, were subtle cracks, as though there was a panel in the statue.

I felt around the cracks, my intuition telling me that the real prize was there, within the panel. How Capano missed it, I had no idea, but there it was!

Several minutes later, my elation turned to dejection. I could find no way to open it. No latch, no button, no lever, nothing. Maybe Capano had seen the panel after all, and simply failed to get it open. In lieu of accessing the treasure within, he simply decided to bury it so no one could have it. That seemed a fitting course of action for the Dark champion.

Which did not tell me how I was going to open it. After several minutes of trying, I ran out of ideas, except a crowbar or hammer, but that would destroy the rest of the statue so I did not want to go there. Frustrated, I stood up from the table and turned toward the condo's kitchenette. I needed another drink.

But as I turned away, I felt a tugging on my chest, something sliding. I looked down and saw the outline of the Light emblem beneath my shirt. Instead of hanging straight down, it hung at an angle - pointing toward the statue.

I hurriedly pulled the emblem out and saw that it, too, was glowing. The starburst symbol unerringly faced the statue no matter which way I turned. I felt a surge of excitement and sat back down at the table. The emblem began pulling toward the statue more forcefully, so I took the necklace off and held it closer. The emblem swung into the statue in the center of the small panel. There was a bright flash of pure white light, dazzling but not stunning, and the panel fell open with an soft CLICK.

I blinked away purplish spots from my eyes and as I removed the panel's contents: a leather-bound book that was held closed by a thong. A symbol I did not recognize, a coat of arms probably, was stamped into the front of the book. As I removed the thong - it was stiff with age - and opened the book, the pages crackled softly. I winced, hoping nothing had been damaged, and slowed down. The pages were yellowing, brittle. Fading letters, written in tight cursive, filled each page.

I recognized enough words from my High School Spanish class to identify the language, but there was no way I was going to be able to translate it. What's more, this thing was several hundred years old. If it was not handled correctly, it could be damaged or destroyed. I needed help.

A quick Google search on my laptop showed me where to go. I gathered up my things and hurried out to the car. A couple hours later, I drove into downtown Charleston and, after weaving through charming tree-lined streets, pulled into a parking garage on Wentworth Street.

The College of Charleston Department of Hispanic Studies advertised itself on its website as the largest organization of its kind in the southeast. They could translate the book if anyone could. On my way into town, I called ahead and found the Department Chair had office hours this afternoon. Pretty lucky, but I was beginning to think luck had nothing to do with it.

As I walked into the Chair's office, I was struck, as I usually am in academic institutions, by the feeling of calm scholarship about the place. I could feel the accumulated knowledge of the place oozing from the very walls.

Professor Miriam Escobar was a greying woman in her mid-50s, wearing jeans and a short-sleeved flowery shirt with a narrow collar. I liked her on sight. She was just finishing up with some students when I knocked on her door. She looked up, an eyebrow quirking upward as she saw me and what I carried.

"You must be the one who called," she said with a wry grin.

Nodding, I waited for the students to leave before stepping into her office, closing the door behind me. After introductions, I placed the statue and book down on her desk and explained quickly where I found it, leaving out the bit about guns and almost getting buried alive. This did not seem the right forum for that sort of discussion.

The Professor's eyebrows lifted again as I finished my story, and she clucked at her teeth with her tongue. "You would be surprised how often this sort of thing happens, Mr. Williams. Well," she said, picking up the book, "let's have a look." She opened the cover and looked inside.

Her eyes widened.

* * * * *

Three weeks later, I watched an interview on Good Morning American on the TV set in my firm's conference room. Giobald Capano, looking the epitome of understated elegance in his simple but expensive clothing, sat in a stuffed chair between Professor Escobar and another academic type, and flashed a winning smile at the anchor's question.

"It goes without saying," he said, his tone pleasant, ingratiating. "When we found the statue on my property, I knew it was important, so I had my associate contact Professor Escobar immediately."

"Where did you find it?"

He shrugged. "I came upon it while digging a swimming pool." He flashed his smile again. "Just dumb luck."

The anchor shook her head, affecting astonishment, then turned to the academic man I did not recognize. "Professor Goldstein, why is this find so significant?"

"Well, quite simply, this completely changes our understanding of early European colonization. Here we have the journal of a Spanish priest who started an parish in South Carolina twenty years before what we thought were the first Europeans to settle in that region."

"And he did it," interjected Professor Escobar, "in a totally different manner than others elsewhere. Rather than taking advantage of the natives or seeking to convert them, he seems to have actually cared about their culture. When the next Europeans arrived, he appears to have gone out of his way to defend the natives from them."

"And paid for it with his life." Professor Goldstein managed to sound grieved by this fact.

The anchor sighed, a convincing expression of sorrow on her face for a moment. Then she looked back at Capano and brightened again. "Now, Mr. Capano, you took things one step further didn't you?"

Capano nodded. "After the professors informed me how important the find was, we realized there were probably more artifacts from the priest's parish on my property." He smiled broadly and managed to look almost angelic. "So I decided to donate that property to the College of Charleston, in the interest of science."

The anchor smiled along with Capano and shook her head. "Truly a generous gesture," she said as she turned to face the camera. "And a fitting cap to a story that sheds new light on a true man of compassion."

The segment ended, going to commercial, and I switched off the TV.

"Well," Jim said from the chair next to me, "it sucks we

lost the Capano account, but I guess you can't fault his reasons."

"No, I guess not."

Jim stood up and clapped me on the shoulder. "Ah well, there's always next time." He strode to the conference room door and looked back at me with a grin. "It makes you feel good, though, doesn't it? To know that even back then there were people who stood up for those who could not defend themselves?"

I nodded. It did, and that was the point, wasn't it? That nice little story might influence someone else to goodness, or just brighten someone's day. It was small, but it was a victory, and who knows what its ultimate impact might be?

Jim left and I leaned back in my chair.

I thought long and hard, during the drive to Charleston, about how to play it, and decided going to the cops would have been useless; there were no witnesses to what happened, no evidence either way. It would be my word against Capano's, and I could easily see how that would turn out. Besides, was not the Light supposed to be the side of forgiveness and compassion?

I smiled, thinking about how it must have galled Capano to find out what happened, especially after the Professors contacted him. Yep, I'm a compassionate man.

About The Author

Michael Kingswood is a lifelong fan of science fiction and fantasy literature. He holds a bachelors degree in Mechanical Engineering as well as a Master of Engineering Management and a Master of Business Administration. By day, he is a professional Naval Officer. He lives with his wife and four children wherever the Navy deems to send them.

Find Michael Kingswood online at:

www.michaelkingswood.com

www.facebook.com/michael.kingswood

twitter.com/michaelkingswd